Night of the Scarab

Night of the Scarab

She shopped and got back to the vehicle Max had arranged for her. The windshield wiper trapped a folded white paper against the glass on the driver's side. Hoping it wasn't a ticket, she plucked away the paper. She opened the door and sank into the driver's seat. She plopped her purse and the pizza box on the passenger's seat. Her hands free, she unfolded the note against the steering wheel with an oddly uneasy breath. Stark black words stared back at her.

Get out! Quickly, she looked up and saw no one, except for an elderly woman pushing an empty cart into the storage rack. Diane locked the car doors from inside and drove out of the parking lot. Her thoughts burst loose, and her pulse flew up as well as her speed on the road. She *was* being threatened. More boldly this time. She was somebody's target.

What They Are Saying About
Night of the Scarab

If you enjoy a cocktail of Egyptian history—mummies, hieroglyphics, and sphinxes—laced with a shot of murder, then this one's for you. Karen Hudgins' *Night of the Scarab* will keep you guessing as P.I. Diane Phipps heads to The Great Sand Dunes National Park in Southern Colorado to find out who killed archeologist Irene Albertine. Is the motive theft, love, or did Irene's tempestuous nature tip somebody over the edge?

—Andrea Barton, Brightside Story Studio, author of *The Godfather of Dance* coming soon from Wings ePress.

The sands of Ancient Egypt and Colorado's Great Sand Dunes mingle in *Night of the Scarab*, the newest installment in the Diane Phipps, P. I. mystery series. I loved following Diane through the twists and turns of her investigation, encountering one suspicious character after another, especially as the tension built and it seemed the only clues she could trust came from her own intuition. Though part of a series, *Night of the Scarab* also reads successfully as a stand-alone novel. Readers are sure to be captivated on multiple levels, from the well-developed characters to the details of Egyptian studies to the intrigue of the mystery itself. I'm looking forward to experiencing more P. I. Phipps mysteries!

—Heather O'Connor, author of *My Watcher's Eyes* and *When No one's Watching*

Irene Albertine and her dad, Max, love everything Egyptian. Many archeological adventures solidified that passion. And when a newly acquired 2500-year-old mummy waited to be unveiled at the Scarab Gala, they couldn't have been more thrilled and excited.

The gala's main function to extract huge contributions for the museum seemed primed to succeed. The ballroom had been transformed into a replica of the tomb where the mummy Set-Nohr had been found.

Those intricate plans dissolved into chaos. Irene's lifeless body tumbled out of the casket when Max and his assistant removed the lid. She'd been murdered.

Who would want to kill Irene? A missing necklace with an attached rare red diamond screamed robbery and suspects were identified. Looked like an open and shut case at first. But the well-respected PI, Diane Phipps, Max had hired was skeptical, and determined to solve the case.

It's a fun trip to southern Colorado for exploring sand dunes, evaluating diverse characters, and following clues to ferret out the true killer.

—J. D. Webb, author of *Incredible Witness*

"If you like murder most foul, ancient Egyptian mummies, priceless necklaces, and a long, slow burn of mystery that flames out in a dark, bottomless pit, then Karen Hudgins' Night of the Scarab is for you. But a note of warning—just when you think you know "whodunit"—you don't. Don't skip ahead; it's worth the wait."

—Gwynne Stanker
Published author, novelist, and short story writer

Clear the day, grab a coffee, and curl up in your favorite chair because a new Diane Phipps P.I. novella is here. Karen Hudgins' *Night of the Scarab* is an electrifying page turner, where Phipps is on the search for a killer. I was hooked from the first word and raced through the pages as I followed the P.I.'s twists and turns, as she unraveled the mystery of 'who killed Irene Albertine.' Along the way I learned a lot about Egyptian history, which was an added bonus. I highly recommend this book as a good read and an exhilarating, challenging new adventure for Diane Phipps. Congratulations, Karen Hudgins, on an excellent new book. Please, don't miss it!

—Suzanne Hurley, Author of the Samantha Barclay Mystery Series

Night of the Scarab

Karen Hudgins

A Wings ePress, Inc.
Mystery Novel

Wings ePress, Inc.

Edited by: Jeanne Smith
Copy Edited by: Christie Kraemer
Executive Editor: Jeanne Smith
Cover Artist: Trisha FitzGerald-Jung
Images from Pixabay

All rights reserved

Names, characters and incidents depicted in this book are products of the author's imagination or are used fictitiously. Any resemblance to actual events, locales, organizations, or persons, living or dead, is entirely coincidental and beyond the intent of the author or the publisher.

No part of this book may be reproduced or transmitted in any form or by any means, electronic or mechanical, including photocopying, recording, or by any information storage and retrieval system, without permission in writing from the publisher.

Wings ePress Books
www.wingsepress.com

Copyright © 2023 by: Karen Hudgins
ISBN 978-1-59088-645-8

Published In the United States Of America

Wings ePress, Inc.
3000 N. Rock Road
Newton, KS 67114

Dedication

For Scott D. Miller

"The number one rule of thieves is that nothing is too small to steal."

—Jimmy Breslin

Prologue

August
Sandy River, CO

Irene Albertine left Egypt excited to be home in time for her father's birthday. On the same day, the long-awaited opening of the Linens of Yesterday Exhibit at Albertine's Center for Egyptian Studies was to happen. Their newest acquisition—the Set-Nohr mummy—would be unveiled during the Night of the Scarab Gala in the evening.

Members of the Osiris Society were set to celebrate Set-Nohr's arrival and Irene's dad's sixty-one years. Except for his travels, Maximilian Albertine had made his home by the Great Sand Dunes in Colorado.

"This is your happy place, isn't it?" she'd asked him one day over lunch at the Sphinx Café.

He gazed out the window. "These dunes take me back to where I've visited so often. Sand, sky, the sun... and where discoveries wait for us to find." And he had. His interest and financial support for the Ra Project in the Valley of the Kings had put his name on the archaeological map. From time to time, Irene had spent days doing brushwork by his side.

To this day, her historical architect father's heart swelled at the sight of a pyramid. Ramesses II, 19th Dynasty, impassioned him most. Set-Nohr was the daughter of a priest who served the pharaoh. Having her at Albertine's seemed right.

Irene's love for ancient Egypt matched Maximilian's. Art was more her game than structures, and she delighted in comparing the art styles between Amenhotep IV and King Tut with her father.

As hoped, she had arrived home yesterday from another extended visit to a promising excavation she was spearheading. What secrets it held were yet to be known.

For now, though, Irene focused on the gala. Three weeks ago, her father approved the formal invitations that were sent out far and wide. A red wax seal imprinted with a scarab was affixed on the back flap.

You Are Invited

The Albertine Center of Egyptian Study and Museum cordially invites you to the Linens of Yesterday Exhibit and Night of the Scarab Gala when you'll meet Set-Nohr, our 2,500-year-old mummy, and her exquisite coffin and funerary artifacts.

Date: August 27
Unveiling: Seven p.m.
Place: Luxor Ballroom
Complimentary lodging on the premises at the Oasis Guest Inn
Looking forward to spending this special evening with you,
Maximilian Albertine,
Sandy River, Colorado
RSVP card enclosed

Late yesterday, Irene had settled into her suite, unpacked, and smiled over how the RSVPs had poured in. A full house was expected. This morning, she fought off a case of the jitters. Things needed to be double-checked. She left her office wearing a navy-blue shirtdress, and her brown hair had been retouched with lowlights. Ready to be impressed, because Albertine's never did anything halfway, she headed for the Ramesses II Wing. Encountering Margaret Callahan, Events Assistant, in the lobby, she slowed.

"Good morning," Margaret recited evenly. "Good to have you back." The woman had a few years on Irene's forty-two. Undoubtedly, her black knit dress slimmed her. Yet, paired with her salt and pepper hair, and tortoise-framed round glasses, she seemed too in charge for Irene's taste. However, Irene silently gave Margaret points for wearing low-heeled shoes for walking around the 60,000-square-foot space. But perfectionist Irene felt it her duty to suggest another dress color later.

"Margaret," she began coolly. "Progress report?"

Margaret raised her chin. "First, I want to say I got your note." Her tone lacked warmth.

Irene averted her gaze. "Now is not the time, Margaret."

"Probably not," she agreed. "So, the ballroom is nearly ready. Table and chair set-ups are finishing as we speak. The stage is set. The problem with the lighting was fixed earlier this morning. The curtain operates quite well. Set-Nohr is in center stage, and she's certainly the star of the show."

Eager to see for herself, Irene said, "I'll check it." The Center was counting on this exhibit launch in further support of its stellar reputation. "Now, about the dinner seating arrangement. I'm to sit at the right of my father. Cedric Hardwick is to sit at his left."

"At the head table, of course," Margaret said.

"Also, today is my father's birthday. I trust you've arranged to supply him with some extra attention?" Her tone of voice conveyed it wasn't a question.

Margaret fielded it well. "Chef is making him a big cake."

Irene nodded. "Not chocolate, and no ice cream."

"Marble cake, I believe." Her hazel eyes shone brightly. "We'll sing."

"Not one note," Irene stressed and adjusted the scarf with its gold printed ankhs scattered over the blue silk. It almost covered her gold cartouche, a gift from her father, with its rare red diamond embedded in the middle. "A toast will be acceptable. And olives. He likes fat ones with pimentos pushing out the end."

Margaret clasped her hands in front of her. "Yes, ma'am."

Irene stepped toward the ballroom. "Now, when my father is offering his talk about his travels, do not ring a bell to signal his time is over. It irritates him."

"Right," Margaret said, following slightly behind her. "We'll not upset Mr. Albertine on his birthday."

"Good idea," Irene warned. "Now, I'm ready to see the ballroom."

Margaret hesitated. "I'm afraid that won't be possible."

Irene straightened her spine. "Not possible? Why not?"

"Security locked it down. No entry except for key personnel until the event."

Irene glared.

"High security due to the mummy," Margaret explained. "Chief of Security's policy."

Irene cried, "That's ridiculous. I have time to preview it now. Call him."

Margaret raised her hands in protest. "That would be insubordination. I already have a black mark for taking a short-cut through the kitchen last week."

Irene sighed and slung a hand at her waist. "Pity."

Margaret acknowledged her with silence.

Irene tapped her foot on the floor. "Who makes up rules like this?"

"Forgive me, ma'am, I'd rather not say."

"Margaret, you know who I am? Without me and my father, none of this would be here, got it? So, get DiNardo on the line right now."

Margaret widened her eyes and pulled a cell phone from her pocket.

Irene turned on her heel and strode further down the corridor toward the Luxor Ballroom. She glanced over her shoulder at Margaret, who clutched her phone at her ear. Reaching the double doors of the ballroom, flanked by towering statues of Ramesses II, Irene stopped. Arms crossed, she waited for Margaret to catch up in less than a minute.

Relief shone on her face. "Security Chief DiNardo's on his way."

"I'll wait. I'm sure you have other things to do," she said, shooing her fingers at Margaret.

Margaret added, keeping her smooth tone. "Oh, reminder of the private photo session with the mummy after the dinner. Enjoy your evening."

Irene nodded vaguely and repeated her go-away gesture, as Margaret issued a slight dip and left. Chief DiNardo, suited and sleek-haired, arrived with a smile pasted on his face.

"Sorry for the inconvenience," he said and produced an oversized key ring. It jangled as he rifled through, finding the right one. "Just taking precautions."

Making no comment, Irene entered the Luxor Ballroom. The hush slowed her pace. Transformed into a replica of one found in the famous pharaoh's tomb, the cavernous space stunned even her. Meticulously hand-painted copies of original reliefs covered the walls. Torch-like sconces flickered between potted palm trees that separated panels of colorful hieroglyphics.

In the dim light, she wended her way between round tables draped in red and blue cloths. She gazed steadily at the stage in front of the ballroom. A thick, red velvet curtain with a gold scarab embossed in the center had been dropped to hide the stage. Behind it Set-Nohr and her coffin was dominating the setting. The slow, steady raising of the curtain tonight would unveil her in full light. Irene's heart thumped.

Eager to see the Set-Nohr closer, she mounted the four steps to the stage and slipped behind the curtain. Mesmerized, she stood in awe. *This*. This was what Irene liked best—time alone for up-close study, photographing, and sketching artful details. As expected, she wasn't disappointed.

Set-Nohr stood tilted upright in a clear acrylic case held in place with colorless rods. An overhead spotlight shone down on her. In its magnificence, her empty coffin was tilted next to her, the painted lid on one side, facing front for the audience to see, and the bottom on the other, with its hieroglyphic inside. The mask on the lid was molded in her likeness. Her round obsidian eyes lined with kohl and hooded with heavy brows stared straight ahead.

The mummy's fifteen-ton stone sarcophagus had been left in Cairo. Luckily, looters had overlooked the treasure inside. Set-Nohr could've been ground up for mummia, a popular ancient medicine. Irene shuddered at the thought.

Sudden footsteps coming from behind Irene jarred her. She spun around.

"Margaret? What're you doing in here?"

She hesitated, then said, "I'm here to talk to you about this note you wrote me." She brandished the paper in front of Irene. "You have no right doing this to me, or your dad."

"Of course I do," Irene seethed. "We take care of each other now. You're not needed... or wanted. So just stop seeing my father."

Margaret stepped closer. "Irene, this is ridiculous. Your dad wants me in his life. We're more than friends. We have plans."

"No, you don't. Get out!" Irene raised her arms and shoved Margaret backwards. The woman almost lost her balance and grabbed the red velvet curtain to steady herself.

"Never. We love each other." She lurched forward and pitched herself shoulder-first into Irene's chest. Irene flew backwards and crumpled to the floor. On the way down, pain shot through her head as it caught the end of Set-Nohr's coffin.

Unknown minutes later, Irene regained consciousness. "Oh, God," she moaned. She reeled from the head pain and struggled to her feet. Margaret was gone. Aghast, she turned toward the steps off the stage as heavy footsteps thudded from behind her. Grabbing her, an assailant hissed, "You! It was YOU!"

"Leave me alone," she cried as a cool moist cloth met her nose and mouth. Clamped in place with strong, gloved fingers, the pressure increased.

Irene gasped, clenched her teeth, and thrust herself backwards. Her attacker held fast and jammed the soaked fabric harder against her mouth.

"Help!" she garbled as her throat tightened. Her knees wobbled, while shock stole her lucidity. Seconds flashed into short, woozy minutes. Her heart thundered as terror weakened her muscle power and senses. Deepening darkness swallowed her consciousness. Slowly, Irene surrendered to the deadly, sweet scent.

One

Atlantic Beach, Florida
A New Client

Two strangers huddled under a black golf umbrella as Diane Phipps opened the outside door of her office. Both men looked agitated. The October torrential rain had moved in about twenty minutes ago. She glanced at the front curb disappearing underwater.

"May I help you?" she asked with mixed feelings. Tropical storm Lia had been heading toward the northeast part of the coast for two days. In readiness, Diane had reset her two appointments. Not expecting company, she wore sweats and let her chestnut hair wander where it may.

"We need you," the older gentleman blurted. His voice, smooth and cultured, was laced with urgency. His faded blue eyes sported wrinkles at their corners, his face tanned. He held himself straight despite the wind, as if he were used to extreme weather.

The younger, more stocky man stepped forward. "What my friend Max means is that we need your services," he said in an English accent and pointed to the shingle by the door. *Diane Phipps, P.I., Appointment preferred.*

"Oh, of course," she said. The black limo parked out front looked like a beached whale. Its headlight beams were shredded by wind and warm rain. Windshield wipers thumped to keep up with the deluge. "Please come in."

She opened the door wider, allowing them to step into the small entryway. The older gentleman lowered the umbrella and shook it. Before entering, he plunged it into the ceramic umbrella stand with flamingos painted on it.

"This way," she said and led the visitors to her office, once a spare bedroom.

Diane centered herself behind her desk. The wood surface was somewhat cluttered this morning. The stapler lay on its side. Her knitting basket, where she kept Pearl her revolver, overflowed with yarn, and paperclips lay scattered about. But the pages in her little notebook had been neatly replaced, ready for details in a new case.

"My, this is really bloody interesting," the Englishman said of the weather, brushing away the water drops falling from his souvenir cap that featured sand dunes. They were much higher than those that lined the beach a few blocks away.

"Unexpected, to say the least," the older gentleman said. "We hardly ever see rain like this out our way, do we, Cedric?" He stood at about six feet tall and his gray hair slipped past his ears to touch the collar of his plaid flannel shirt. An ancient Egyptian Eye of Horus and the letters ACES & M beneath were embroidered on his tan vest, which almost matched his khaki pants.

"Hardly," he replied and offered, "I'm Cedric Hardwick, and this is—"

"Maximilian Albertine," the older man cut in. "We've no appointment, but we are here on urgent business."

Diane's curiosity flared. She dragged a wooden library chair and put it next to the overstuffed yellow chintz chair where clients usually sat. Mr. Albertine chose the chintz chair which directly faced Diane's desk. He didn't sink deep into the comfort as many others had done. Instead, he sat perched at the front edge, his long legs crossed at his ankles. He folded his hands on his knees. He seemed a man used to being in charge. Mr. Hardwick took the wood chair, as Diane tucked strands of her hair behind her ears.

"Has something of interest happened?" she asked Mr. Albertine.

"Most definitely," he said, his distraught, harried expression rising. "My daughter... my daughter Irene was murdered." Tears welled. "I want help finding out who did this. Our local law office is small. Sheriff Cotton is doing his best, and he thinks some jewel thieves did it."

Diane leaned forward. She said softly, "I'm sorry for your loss." She cringed inside over her words. They always seemed so inadequate. "How long ago did she pass away?"

"Two months," Cedric put in.

Maximilian cleared his throat. "I want you to hire you. I'm well-prepared to make your time in Sandy River worth your while."

Diane opened her computer and, before accepting a new client, she checked her schedule and Tom's schedule. More and more she was trying to synchronize hers with her husband's. She was also trying to stick closer to home with her next case. Lord knew there were enough heinous transgressions happening in the state. But the gentlemen's urgency drew her in.

"I'd like to know more. Where's Sandy River?"

Cedric pointed to his cap. "It's a small community next to The Great Sand Dunes National Park in Southern Colorado, near Alamosa."

Diane raised an eyebrow. "You've come from there to see me?"

Mr. Albertine explained, "Cedric and I attended a symposium on Egyptian art at the Cummer Museum of Art in Jacksonville. Irene had tickets, and we used them. You're a short skip and a jump away."

"True, I am," she said as Tom, her husband, walked into the room.

"Good morning, gentlemen," he greeted, and then quickly turned to Diane. Raising a forefinger, he said, "Excuse me, I need the binoculars. There's a waterspout by the bridge." He stepped to a shelf and picked them up.

Diane made quick introductions.

"I say, sir. A waterspout?" Cedric asked.

Diane swiveled her chair around to see out the window. She opened the flat-slatted hurricane shades without jarring the orchid plant on the sill. Sure enough, they could all spot the long, wide tower of water being sucked up higher than the Intracoastal Waterway bridge. Mesmerized, she and the others watched it die down to nothing in moments.

Mr. Albertine stirred. His eyes sad. "Gone, just like my Irene." He gazed at Diane. I want you to come... now."

Tom straightened and shot Diane a quick frown. "Not a good idea." He hooked a thumb over his shoulder toward the window. "A second rain band is due in an hour."

Diane pursed her lips and nodded at her prospective new client. "Tom has a point."

Cedric exchanged wary glances with Mr. Albertine. "She has a point."

Albertine harrumphed.

Tom put aside the binoculars and asked, "I'm curious. How did you hear about my wife?"

Mr. Albertine shifted in the chair to face him better. "Do you fly much?"

Tom scratched his eyebrow. "Quite a bit."

"Then of course you've probably noticed the complimentary flight magazine for passengers to read?"

Tom hedged. "Not how I fly, but go on, please."

"On our flight here, I read an article, '"The Best Of'." It gave suggestions about who or what in the country was 'The Best' at a service or practice. Like the best hotels in the country, best steakhouses, best eye surgeons, best colleges, and so on. Near the end of the article was a list of best investigators or detectives for people who need this kind of service and talent. Ms. Phipps, your wife, was listed."

"First up," Cedric said with a smile.

Diane widened her eyes. "I'm in an airline magazine?"

Tom chuckled. "You're going places, and I'm not surprised."

Mr. Albertine said, "I strive for excellence, and you are touted to be one of the best, so... Also, the article mentioned that you like museums."

Diane leaned back in her chair. "I do."

Albertine pushed himself to his feet. "Ms. Phipps, I own a museum, one devoted to ancient Egyptian culture and artifacts. Someone took my daughter's life and attempted to ruin my center and museum. I implore you to take my case."

She rechecked her schedule, looked out the window and at Tom, and looked back at Mr. Albertine. The schedule screen was open for business. The view out the window promised a rough flight, even a cancellation, but eventually, the rain would end.

Tom shot her a glance with a serious glint in his eyes. "You and Pearl have a good trip," while Mr. Albertine sat with hope in his eyes.

She reached for her notebook and opened it to a fresh page. "Let me ask you, Mr. Albertine, I take it that you were closest to your daughter?"

He nodded. "I was. She had no husband, no sister, and her mother passed away three years ago."

Diane noted the facts. "I see." Tilting her head to one side, she asked, "So, who do you *think* would've killed her?"

"Here, here," Cedric said sharply. "Perhaps Max would rather say in private?"

Still standing, the museum owner paced around the yellow chair and stopped behind it. Resting his hands on the top of the back cushion, he locked eyes with Diane. "If I knew I wouldn't need you. I simply don't know." That stated, he waited for her answer.

Diane rose to her feet, stepped around her desk, and proffered her hand to Mr. Albertine. He came around the chair in haste and shook her hand.

"I'll come," Diane said. "After the rain lets up."

Cedric slapped his knee with his hand. "There, there." Looking at Tom, he added, "We'll take good care of her, sir."

Tom flat out grinned. "You guys have that the other way around."

Two

Maximilian and Set-Nohr

Two days later, Diane arrived at the Colorado Springs airport. Maximilian led her to a black limousine, apparently his preferred mode of transportation. She sat in the back seat with him as his driver drove south on I-25.

"I'm exceptionally grateful you're here," Maximilian said to Diane. "The whole affair over losing Irene almost did me in. No new developments. Sheriff Cotton is still investigating Irene's death."

Diane turned toward him. "I'm sure this is very difficult for you. Both Tom and I are moved by your loss. I'll do what I can to get to the bottom of it."

Maximilian, wearing dark pants, a smooth gray sweater topped off with a finely woven red scarf, raised his cane in acceptance. "I've spoken to Sheriff Cotton about you. He regrets not being able to close my case. Nobody seems to have a real answer."

Diane unbuttoned her jacket. "These things take time."

"I suppose." He paused, and then, "The Nile Suite has been reserved for you for as long as you need. As agreed, I'm covering your fee and expenses, and a car is waiting for you."

Diane smiled inside. Her need for digging up truth was exceeding her need for beach walks with her bare feet in the sand. It seemed ironic that so many miles away she would still be around sand. Unlike in Atlantic Beach, where wood crossovers protect the dunes and their fragile ecosystems, she could walk freely on these dunes.

Maximilian cleared his throat. "Sheriff Cotton wants to meet with you tomorrow morning. He's eager to brief you."

Good news, Diane thought and settled further into the seat. Things went easier if teamwork was involved for investigations. "For now, a good place to start is for you to tell me what happened. I mean, about when and where her body was found. Who was around, and—"

"A *lot* of people were around," he said heavily. "And at the wrong time. It's not the best publicity for my Center."

"Hmm. I see. Also, who liked her and who didn't. Details like that, please. Everything is important."

Maximilian pushed the button to slide up the glass pane between the front and back seats of the vehicle for privacy. He leveled a serious gaze on her. "I'm considering putting up reward money in addition to bringing you on board."

Diane opened her travel bag and pulled out her notebook. "Your prerogative. Let's begin."

"First, I want to say that Irene could be a difficult woman. Not spiteful, but she was prickly. Most will agree she wasn't a warm, fuzzy person. So her friends list was short. But she got things done. Good things, like helping me acquire Set-Nohr for our collection at the museum."

"Set-Nohr?"

Maximilian raised an eyebrow. "Oh, yes. Set-Nohr is a mummy and our newest acquisition. Her father served Ramesses II, Pharaoh, during the nineteenth dynasty. He built more temples along the Nile to please the gods than any other ruler in ancient Egypt. With my background, I feel most connected to him."

He paused and reached into his pocket and pulled out a business card. Handing it to her, he said, "My father was a very established architect. I went to school and joined his firm in Denver. I quickly became fascinated with pyramids and how they were built. It all became a passion, really. The more I could learn about ancient Egypt the better. So, I followed my dad's advice and pursued explorations on site in Thebes, Memphis, and The Valley of the Kings. Now, it's all about the Center, not much exploring these days."

It made sense to Diane as she checked his card. Maximilian J. Albertine, Historical Architect, Founder, Albertine Egyptian Center and Museum, Sandy River, Colorado.

"Interesting," she said, awed and with growing curiosity.

He went on. "Early on, Irene often went with me, made her own connections, and more recently took care of administrative tasks for acquisitions without complaint. My interest in temple chambers and pyramids rubbed off on her." He leaned forward and pulled two bottled waters from a built-in cooler. "Water?" he asked. "Keeping hydrated at higher altitudes is important."

She accepted one, unscrewed the cap, and sipped. "What did Irene's mother do?"

He ran his hand down his jaw. "Ava and I weren't a good match. I was away a lot."

Diane kept her eyes on her notebook page. "Oh?"

"She was a textile designer. Never wanted to leave her studio, except for trade shows. He looked out the window as mountains rolled by. "That's Cheyenne Mountain over there," he threw in. "And she didn't like sifting through dust or digging dirt, or taking long trips. We stuck together for Irene."

"Couples do that," Diane mentioned lightly.

"We divorced about three years ago. After that, Irene moved from Denver to be with me in Sandy River."

Diane listened with respect. "You mentioned your wife passed away?"

He finished drinking his water and set the bottle aside. "After our divorce she established a deep relationship with alcohol. Ran her Mini-Cooper into a guardrail up in St. Vrain Canyon. Fatal."

Diane gave him a minute.

"By the way," he said, "We don't own mummies; we are only their caretakers."

"Only caretakers," she repeated, sensing that she wasn't only going to investigate a homicide case; she was enroute to learning a lot about ancient Egypt.

Her client's shoulders drooped, and he loosened his scarf. "The day of Irene's murder was the worst day of my life."

Diane said quietly, "I'm truly sorry you're going through this."

Maximillian looked out the car window for a few miles, then, "I have no idea who took Irene from me. If I did, they'd be incarcerated by now."

"That's where I come in," Diane said. "So, go on... more about that day. I'm listening."

Three

That Day

A few miles flew by until Maximilian said, "It was my birthday, August twenty-seventh. I was in the mood for celebrating it, and the unveiling of Set-Nohr as a permanent part of our Linens of Yesterday Exhibit. A big evening gala, Night of the Scarab, was planned. Invitations were sent, and we even opened it to those with interests in Egypt. More than a hundred guests were expected.

"The day before, Irene arrived from a long trip to Egypt. She'd been going over more often since last year and had sent antiquities and artifacts back for our museum and the gift shop. I was delighted she was home.

"The morning of the Gala, Cedric and I took a walk on the dunes, as we often did. He's an Egyptologist and a major collector. We reminisced how we'd met in Thebes. We'd hit it off. I'd invited him to be part of our visiting faculty here at the Center. An asset, mind you.

"After Cedrick and I returned from our walk, Irene texted me that copies of her book, *A Compendium of Egyptian Art*, had arrived. There were enough for one book to be placed on each guest's chair."

"A lovely touch and generous," Diane said, looking up from her notes.

"She also reminded me of the VIP photo shoot with the mummy after the unveiling. It would be used for the next issue of the Osiris Society newsletter and the local newspaper." He pulled his cellphone from his pocket, scrolled, and gazed at the message on the screen. "This was our last communication."

He drifted off in thought for another moment. "Seven o'clock arrived, and almost everyone was seated in the Luxor Ballroom. But Irene wasn't at the head table with Cedric and me. I texted her, but no answer. We waited a bit, and then we had to proceed. We just had to. And that's when everything happened..."

Diane sat still. Maximilian's face tightened with sorrow. He choked up. "*Irene was gone...*" His cane shook under his grip.

"Gone?" She needed more.

"Murdered." He barely squeaked out the word.

Diane let her pen rest and briefly closed her eyes. Hearing family recollections of finding a loved one dead never got easier. Sometimes, she resisted her own tears. "We can talk later, if you wish."

He dug for a handkerchief and dabbed a watery eye.

"Thank you, Ms. Phipps. It still hits me hard."

If she were in his shoes, she'd feel the same way. "Mourning is a tough road."

Her client fell quiet again. She let her own gaze roam out the limo window. Rolling hills took over covered with tan grasses. Cottonwood trees boasted golden leaves that contrasted with a brilliant blue sky.

Maximilian stirred back into conversation. "Pardon me. Irene was supposed to give the opening welcome, but Margaret stepped in for her instead. Applause broke out, and I took the stage. Let me say, it was a grand set-up. The red curtain rose on cue. The lights came up, but..."

"But what?"

"When I checked on her earlier in the day, Set-Nohr was propped up dead center on the stage. She shone like an ancient star. She was wrapped in aged linen that looked like it was tea stained. She was well-cared for. Due to her position when she was alive, she was given a costly mummification. Nothing was spared for helping her into the Afterlife. The shabtis, amulets, and canopic jars that had been buried with her were on display in front of the stage. All was set for our guests to admire." His voice cracked. "But, but... when the curtain came up at the gala, the arrangement on the stage had been changed. Set-Nohr was still in the middle with a soft light on her, as we planned. But the lid to her inner coffin had been put back onto the empty bottom. No one could see the beautiful hieroglyphics on the interior. I was perturbed.

"Sorry, folks," I said into the microphone. "We have a malfunction. Cedric, will you come up and help me?"

"And he did," Diane said, picturing it all.

"Of course. The two of us could lift the top from the bottom without breaking off the wooden tabs to keep it in place, and then everyone could see inside. But we didn't have gloves at hand, so dear Margaret ran and got us some from the archivist office." His lips quivered. "Cedric and I set to work on making the amends. We lifted carefully and with some effort while the audience sat respectfully quiet and sipped libations. It took one big push, and we got the lid safely off its base and down to the floor.

"Then came the screams. From the whole room. As I jerked around, my Irene fell forward out of the coffin onto the stage! Lifeless, crumpled, and eyes wide open. A white cloth had been stuffed into her mouth."

Diane stiffened. Words almost failed her. "Oh, how horrible." Even bizarre, she thought.

"Complete chaos broke out after that. Never heard a woman scream like Margaret. The photographer called DiNardo in security. He arrived quickly and used nine-one-one. The fire truck, ambulance, and sheriff came right after. The ballroom doors were shut and no one was allowed to leave. Cedric helped me off the stage. My Osiris peeps were besides themselves in shock and dismay."

Diane's thoughts briefly shifted to what customarily followed in such disruptions. First responders trying to organize and secure the space which had suddenly become a crime scene. Multiple people reacting, probably, and mindlessly ruined evidence. "A white cloth?" she murmured.

Maximilian's complexion almost matched one. "Yes. A white napkin—from our Sphinx Café."

"She was smothered?"

"She technically died from respiratory failure from a heavy-duty, contaminated dose of chloroform. The medical examiner found the cloth was soaked with it, and it killed her."

Diane shook her head. "Unbelievable and unusual. Chloroform. Where did someone get that?"

"The medical examiner suggested it was probably a homemade batch that went bad."

Diane just learned something new. Primed for seeing the Luxor Ballroom herself and going over crime scene reports, she looked forward more than ever to meeting the local sheriff. They already had something in common. Wanting to find a murderer.

Four

Sheriff Cotton and the Federal Marshal

Diane rose early and had two hours free before her appointment with Sheriff Jerry Cotton. She found Route 160 that led to the entrance of The Great Sand Dunes National Park. Within minutes, she parked and walked over the shallow trickle of Medano Creek, created by runoff from the Sangre de Cristo Mountains. Luckily, water didn't seep into her tooled leather shoes. The October breeze refreshed her as she stepped onto the dry sand on the other side of the creek.

From first sight, Diane had wanted to connect with the dunes, way higher and massive than those she was used to along the Atlantic Ocean. A map showed the highest was Star Dune, at about 730 feet.

A pocket of paradise, the sand and sky filled her vision. Mt. Blanca rested majestically behind her. Her steadily made footprints disturbed the wind patterns sculpted on the surface of the sand. Her breath ran low... really fast. She stopped to catch it and drink from the water bottle the concierge at the Oasis Guest Inn suggested she bring. The moment gave her the chance to absorb pure Nature. Better yet, she could think without interruption. *Who could kill Irene Albertine? Why leave her body in such a unique, public way?*

Looking about, she saw other visitors strung out on the sand. Some had hiked up and far enough away they appeared to be blotches of color bobbing around, disappearing, and coming back again like small boats in a red flag ocean beyond Jax Pier.

Families, solo hikers, and couples were exploring at will. Time seemed to fade away as she took on climbing again, making very slow progress. She regretted Tom wasn't with her. Even he, in his buff shape, would be challenged. Walking on sand took twice the effort.

Checking the time on her phone after a few snappies, she turned around. She spotted two figures walking arm-in-arm out across the sand. The man, wearing a dark jacket and a red scarf, slowed and kissed the woman on her forehead. Her denim duster fluttered in the breeze. They held her attention for a moment, and then Diane began walking again back down the slope, thinking it was nice to see people share affection out on the dunes.

~ * ~

Fresh off the dunes, Diane walked into the Sandy River Sheriff's Office. Sheriff Jerry Cotton met her in the small reception room. Gray-haired, he wore a tan uniform with his badge clipped to the pocket of his shirt. "Good to have you with us."

She reciprocated his pleasantness.

"C'mon back," he gestured for her to follow him. "Someone's here for you to meet."

Diane summoned her professional smile and entered the sheriff's small office. It was stripped down, functional, with a tad of Old West. A collection of sheriff's badges framed on a wall with an old holster and a Colt .45 mounted next to them finished off the effect. Two color photographs of dunes added local charm. One dusty window faced out onto the dirt parking lot. The brick library building stood on the other side.

A man rose from the second chair in the room. Dressed in a gray suit, white shirt, and plain tie, he looked very "government." Probably six-foot, light brown hair buzzed short, hazel eyes that kept their distance. He exerted little movement.

"This is Federal Marshal Buck Dawson," the sheriff said. "He's also here regarding the Albertine case."

Diane shook hands briefly and sat on the other chair parked right in front of Sheriff Cotton's desk. "I'm here for my client Maximilian Albertine," she told Dawson.

He gave her a nod. "I'm here for case number CO25689713. Grand theft of a gold necklace owned by homicide victim Irene Albertine."

Diane shifted her gaze to Sheriff Cotton, who filled her in. "Mr. Dawson is here following a tip about two fugitive jewel thieves. Their last job produced a dead man."

Dawson said, "Shot in his bed in Baltimore."

"They've expanded their repertoire?" Diane asked.

Dawson smirked and went on. "Warrants issued. They were arraigned and skipped. They're believed to have been seen in this area."

Sheriff Cotton leaned back in his chair, which squeaked, and rested his booted right foot on a bottom drawer.

Diane repeated, "Fugitive jewel thieves here at the Sand Dunes."

Dawson slid her a vague side glance. "You're the P.I.?"

"Florida-based," she confirmed. She dug a card out from her bag, and her little notebook. Handing him her card, she said, "Looks like I might not be here very long."

Sheriff Cotton raised his hand. "Hold on. Nothing is settled about this case. But the marshal here has a viable motive for Irene's murder."

Buck straightened his tie. "Simple theft for a rare, super expensive chunk of jewelry." His voice deep, he explained, "Raphael Franklin and his accomplice Zelda Martin, aka Lady Sticky Fingers, work as a team. They crash posh events where affluent guests wear their best threads and jewels. One was to be held here recently. We think they might've been on hand for the job."

The sheriff confirmed. "Everyone showed up, but the event didn't happen. It was scheduled at the Albertine Egyptian Center and Museum."

Listening, Diane tapped her finger on her notebook. Her intuition didn't tingle over the marshal's theory. "What other motives have come to mind?" she asked Sheriff Cotton.

"Nothing conclusive, and no prime suspect. No prints," he said. He dropped his foot to the floor, opened a drawer, and handed her a fat file stuffed with reports. "These are for you. See what you make of it all, then we'll talk."

She accepted the file and laid it in her lap. "How long are you here for?" she asked Dawson.

"Until I'm directed elsewhere or apprehend the fugitives."

"Hmm. And you think when Irene Albertine resisted, they killed her?"

"Classic grab and run... that went wrong."

"Makes sense to me," Sheriff Jerry said. "Quick and dirty. Nothing else points to it."

"Very dirty," Diane mused aloud. "I'll begin reading these tonight. Meet some people. And I want to tour the crime scene."

"That all can be arranged," he said. "See Albertine staff about the Luxor Ballroom."

"Have you ever met the victim?" she asked the sheriff.

"Hadn't the pleasure," he said. "But Irene was known in these parts. Had her fingers in some pies, and she was the sole heir to the Albertine architecture fortune."

Dawson threw in, "Albertine's could afford red diamonds. One carat is worth a million."

The sheriff winced.

"The necklace is still missing?" she asked.

Dawson replied flatly, "We find Franklin and Martin, we find it."

Diane looked up from her notebook. "Simple, eh?"

"That's what I'm here for," Dawson said.

"Did the victim have a will?" Diane wanted to know.

"Maximilian is her beneficiary," the sheriff said.

Dawson interjected, "She was forty-two, in good health. She didn't expect to die."

"Who saw the victim last?"

Sheriff Dawson said, "From all accounts, a staffer, Margaret Callahan, and security officer DiNardo. They left her alone in the ballroom. But other folks were in and out for setting up things for the event."

Diane listed Callahan and DiNardo in her notebook while the sheriff drank some coffee.

"How about evidence?" Diane asked.

"Not much. Hold on." Sheriff Cotton got up from his chair and left the room.

Dawson cleared his throat. "Ma'am, this case is more about what *wasn't* left at the scene. Namely, a necklace."

Diane stretched out a bit and crossed her legs at her ankles. "What kind of necklace?"

"A gold Egyptian cartouche with a fat red diamond in the middle."

"I see." His description matched what Mr. Albertine had mentioned.

Sheriff Cotton returned with a box of evidence bags. "Not much, but this is what we have. Except for the mummy. We have no room to store a damned mummy and her box. They're locked up at the museum."

Diane straightened and leaned forward. "I've never seen a mummy—in person, that is."

"She's turned black," Sheriff Cotton began. "From the salt they used in mummification. Hollow cheeks... sharp nose. Her teeth lasted but are black like she is. Arms are crossed like this with palms up." He demonstrated and sat back down.

Buck added more. "She's geometrically wrapped with one long strip of old linen, layered from head to toe. She's eyeless. Dusty thick hair. Height, five feet one inch. Medium build. About one hundred twenty pounds. Last seen in about two thousand five hundred B.C. Place of death: unknown." He paused. "Max Albertine gave me a complimentary showing."

Sheriff Cotton finished, "She's not a Jane Doe mummy. Her name is in hieroglyphics on her feet casing."

Diane soaked it all up. She lifted each bag... four of them... and scrutinized each. "A button? Possibly ivory, and carved. She guessed from a sweater or shirt. One side was brown and the front was cream colored. The napkin from the Sphinx Café. Some sand. Irene's clothes and a pair of earrings. How about crime scene photos, videos?"

Sheriff Cotton handed her a thumb drive he lifted from the top tray of his in-box. "All on here."

Diane thanked him and closed her notebook. "I have enough for now."

She was eager for tonight, and after she got back to the Nile Suite to set up the portable whiteboard she used for untangling cases. Her colored markers waited, as did her laptop for writing her own reports for her Case Closed file. It was old school, she knew, but none of it let her down. Eventually, she would type in one name...

Five

Meeting Locals

For now, Diane wanted to explore Sandy River and get the lay of the local land. She drove through the community of eighteen hundred people, up and down scant roads, and sighted landmarks. Noon hit, and she stopped for lunch at Millie's. The parking lot showed strong patronage and getting a table took twelve minutes. The table was rectangular, wood, and meant for six. Scalloped-edged paper placements assigned eating space. Two other diners sat at the other end from her.

The man, wearing a dark green shirt, jeans, boots, and a tan windbreaker nodded. She smiled briefly and perused the menu. Hunger made her pick a bowl of tomato soup and a grilled cheese sandwich. The second person, a woman dressed for success (or because it was Sunday?) gazed at her with interest.

Since Diane wasn't a local and was wearing a surf shop t-shirt, she earned second looks from the couple. The guy in the shirt confirmed her hunch. He raised his water glass and asked, "Are you passing through? Visiting the Dunes before it gets cold?"

Diane moistened her dry lips, rarely a problem in Florida. "Sure."

"I'm Karl, and this is Peggy. Welcome to town."

Peggy tilted her head. "The Information Center out on Route 160 might be of use to you during your visit. My sister Pam works the morning shift."

Diane, grateful for the reception, said, "I might stop by. This is a very unique area."

Peggy dabbed her mouth with a napkin and said, "It usually is nice and quiet around here." She looked meaningfully at Karl. "But things are... a little shaken up right now."

"How so?" Diane asked, making polite small talk.

"We've had a serious crime," Karl said gravely. "A couple of months ago."

Diane let it ride except to say, "I'm sorry to hear."

"Anyway," Peggy began, "If you're here long, there's a good gym that's open to everybody. Do you like to go to the gym?"

"Not usually, but I might give it a try."

"Ahh," Karl said. "You're in town on business?"

Diane hesitated. Keeping a low profile always worked better for sleuthing about. "Dunes are of interest," she said lightly and dipped her spoon into her soup.

Peggy went on, "The gym's at Albertine's. Open exercise class three mornings a week, at nine-thirty. Lunch at the Sphinx Café is the best."

Diane gave her a smile as Karl put down his coffee mug. "Not many people come here for business," he said offhandedly. "Maybe for working at the Dunes, or they're geologists, or potato farmers, ranching, or something. Most folks are on their way to Alamosa and points west."

Peggy said, "Except for when the media and investigators were showing up. So, traffic was up for a while at the four-way stop by the church."

The mention of other investigators tripped Diane's curiosity switch, but she offered no comment. Café curtains hung close to her shoulder. She sat tall enough to peek over them to view the parking lot outside. The sheriff's car pulled into the lot. Sure enough, he'd stop by her table to chat. She considered paying up and leaving so as not to draw any more attention.

While he strode into Millie's, Peggy leaned forward and lowered her voice almost to a whisper. "We've had a murder. Most awful thing ever."

A silent beat followed as Diane opened a pack of crackers.

"Upsetting, I'm sure," she said. "Did you know the person who died?"

"Oh, yes," Peggy said in a hush. "It's not nice to cast shade on the dead, but some think Irene Albertine had it coming."

Karl gave her arm a bump with his elbow. "What she means is that we know most people around here, and... and that lady was hard to get to know."

"Hard to get to know," Peggy echoed as Sheriff Cotton slowed by their table.

He tipped his hat. "Hello, Ms. Phipps," he said amicably. "Out and about? You've picked a good place for lunch. It's the social crossroads of town. There's pizza, darts, and music on Friday nights."

Diane lifted her spoon at him. "Good to know." People relaxed and talked more freely in places like this, which could prove useful in the days to come.

Karl looked up at the sheriff and said, "Say, Jerry, how's it going with that case?"

The sheriff removed his hat and held it in front of him. "Not at liberty to say, but we'll figure it out." He took two steps and turned to Diane. "I need to see you."

"Sure. When I'm finished here."

He moved away and resettled at a back corner table.

Meanwhile, Peggy's eyes widened. "You're here about that murder, aren't you?"

Diane granted her a light shrug. "Not to be advertised, please."

Karl assured her, "Your secret is safe with us."

"Much appreciated," she said, not believing it much. Small community news grew and spread by the minute.

Peggy reached over and patted Diane's hand. "I'm glad you're here, sweetie. Even if it was Irene Albertine who died, we don't need people to stay away. We're a good town."

Diane blinked. "I'm sure." Finishing her soda, she probed, "So, you weren't fond of Irene?"

Peggy raised her chin. "I wasn't very much. She could be very rude."

"Not a people person," Karl threw in. "She knew her place and reminded everyone. Thing is, the big draw here is the sand dunes, not that study center she and her father opened up."

Peggy said, "I've seen her eating in here, and she left no tip for Rachel."

"She was picky. Complained about how potatoes were touching the green beans on her plate."

Diane shook her head. Irritating form on Irene's part, but no reason for murder. Still, it was important to learn what people thought of Irene. This was her first report of solid criticism. Backed up Max Albertine's honest description of his daughter—in a word: prickly. Diane couldn't help wondering why such an accomplished, financially secure woman with a strong future would be so cranky.

Finished eating, and ready to explore more of the community, Diane excused herself, shook hands, and headed to Sheriff Cotton's table.

"You're fraternizing with the locals?" he asked.

"A girl gets hungry," she said. "And I found out the victim wasn't very popular with some folks."

"I've heard, and that angle has been well investigated."

Diane listened. *No motive.* But had every stone been turned?

"Nope, no motive," he said. "Just not irritated enough to turn to rage." He unwrapped flatware tucked inside a paper napkin, and he didn't offer for her to sit.

"You needed to see me?"

"Here's an update. Buck Dawson confirms the jewel thieves were here, getting gas, actually, two days before the murder. Got a positive ID from a station attendant at Wilbur's. Buck showed him that photo he carries around in his pocket, and bingo."

Diane eyed him curiously. "So you think that sews up this case?"

Sheriff Cotton winced. "Until either you or I find out different."

"Any witnesses come forward?" she asked, feeling brave.

"Not a one," he said with a sigh.

"Have a confession?" she pressed.

"Never mind," he said and raised his hands in defense. "But we need to cut Buck some slack. He's been rounding up fugitives for eighteen years."

Diane held her tongue, then, "I'll remember that."

Looking satisfied, he slurped his coffee. "What we have here is a theft with homicide attached. That's it," he staunchly contended. "It's just a matter of tracking down that sticky finger couple."

Admittedly, Diane wished she could go home sooner than later. She missed breakfasts with Tom. But her contract with Mr. Albertine was more than an agreement on paper and a check. It was raw commitment and her professional promise. She had to see this through until the correct arrest was made. It was the hallmark of her sleuthing style and commitment.

She waved a finger at Sheriff Cotton. "With all due respect, my hunch is this case is a pre-meditated homicide. From the timing and the manner in which the victim was killed, I believe her killer was making a statement. Jewel thieves wouldn't care. They'd break and enter, or attack, snatch, and run."

Sheriff Cotton narrowed his eyes at her. She found no contempt in them. Only hope.

"About your hunch?" he said slowly. "Find us proof, girl."

Six

Cedric Dishes

That night, Diane curled up on the couch in the Nile Suite. The sheriff's reports covered her lap and part of the coffee table. Luckily, she was a fast reader of the typewritten incident reports that had started out in deputies' handwriting. She plowed through half of them and made herself some tea.

She next transferred some notes into her little notebook, like names she'd gleaned from the sheriff's pages. They'd come in handy for quick reference and setting up interviews of her own. Some would say the task sounded tedious.

But Diane looked at ferreting out murderers as a great pursuit. Each person she met connected to a case colored her world. Unsavory as some could be, they were portals into a victim's life. All she had to do was enter them, learn more, and put two and two together.

Still, her work was cut out for her, and she turned back to the overview of what had happened on the Night of the Scarab Gala. She read some of it aloud, as she being alone, it was very quiet.

"Called by the nine-one-one dispatcher, Sheriff Cotton arrived first with deputies in tow. The quick-acting guard had shut down the Luxor Ballroom. He shuffled the VIPs and Mr. Albertine to a table near the portable bar. Their names and contact information were collected by Deputy Larson, listed on page two.

"Approximately six minutes after the sheriff's arrival, an ambulance and fire truck reported for service. EMTs assisted those in shock. Mr. Albertine was assisted by friend Cedric Hardwick. In lieu of crime scene unit technicians, Deputies Beard, Wooley, and Gray took photos, measured, and sketched the entire room, including the stage, left and right wings, backstage, and the storage area beneath it... and the victim. K-9 Jasper sniffed and followed perp's trail out the back door behind the stage, and abruptly stopped in parking lot. ID techs from Alamosa dusted for prints; negative presence on stage."

Diane rubbed her eyes and gazed again at the laptop resting next to her on the couch. She'd uploaded the photo file from the jump drive the sheriff had given her. Irene Albertine's ruined body filled the screen. There was no blood. Her lifeless eyes wide open, dulled by death at approximately at six-thirty p.m., according to the medical examiner.

"Who did she see?" Diane whispered to herself, immersed in the aftermath of murder.

Aftermaths told stories. Oh, how she yearned to know this one. Was it someone with a grudge? Short-term or long? Had Irene stepped on someone's toes too hard, causing the person to snap? Or, was it really someone who had cultivated a distinct taste for expensive gems?

A bruise, in the shape of the end of a fat thumb, had appeared on her cheek by photo time. "Gloves were used," Diane figured. *The killer came dressed for the occasion of murder,* she wrote in her book. *Not a spontaneous, drop-in heinous act.*

One thing for sure, the killer had familiarity with the scene, set-up, and schedule. In her estimation, the perp had walked into the Luxor Ballroom with a reason to kill. Buck's jewel thief motive almost went up in smoke before her eyes, *except* high-end heists took just as much planning and clever preparation. Had Raphael and his gal pal cased out Albertine's Egyptian Center and Museum in advance? Equipped with chloroform, had they really intended to subdue her, and their plan went wrong?

To Diane's mind, a lot of questions needed to be answered. Only digging for truth and time would tell if Buck's theory was indeed fact. Undeterred, she checked the names of those whom the sheriff had interviewed. Further into the reports, she found accounts of difficulties several folks had had with Irene at the Center. She intended to find out why. And then, there was Cedric Hardwick, Maximilian's good friend. Of all, he would likely know the Albertines most closely. Had he ever run across something peculiar in their lives? Surely, spending some time with him could yield clues.

Even so, Diane was sure that, as in most cases, the killer would slip up. Make a noticeable mistake that exposed a motive and gave away their identity. She just needed to be on hand for catching the moment and exploring things enough to reveal it was the tip of a destructive iceberg.

~ * ~

A phone call to Mr. Hardwick landed Diane an appointment. His office was located in "Professor Row" at the Center. He taught modules on Tut and Cleopatra and Khufu, quite a broad range in time. She knocked on the windowless door and entered upon hearing, "Come in, please."

The room was square with one window that gave a view of the dunes. Wall posters of Egyptian art and artifact replicas took visitors back to ancient Egypt. Authentic antiquities were displayed in a glass cabinet.

She gave him her name and said, "Thank you for your time."

"Cedric Hardwick, at your service." He grasped her hand in a solid shake. "Come, have a seat. Max is very pleased... better yet, relieved... that you've agreed to take this case. He's losing faith in the local law."

Diane settled in a padded library chair. "Nice to see you again... in drier weather," she said as he rearranged books on his desk, with the largest on the bottom and smallest on top. He looked more relaxed than he had in her Florida office.

"Pardon me," he said. "I'm preparing a reading list for my class on Cleopatra in two weeks." He sighed. "It's a bit of a chore."

Diane opened her notebook. "I'm sure, Professor Hardwick."

He chuckled. "Cedric, just Cedric. Less formal here at Albertine's. But very respectful of the antiquities and artifacts. Those are what makes this place tick... and the field trips to Cairo and surrounds." His grey eyes twinkled.

She suppressed a laugh. "And surrounds?"

Cedric raised a forefinger. "Yes, madam. We visit Saqqara and Alexandria. Three weeks, with papers due after our return. Or the program students don't get their certificates."

While he spoke, Diane scanned the few framed photographs of him standing or kneeling with small groups in front of spectacular Egyptian stone landmarks. A printed card at the bottom of each identified the site and the year.

Looking closer, she recognized one of the other people. Her portrait was hanging in the lobby with a black ribbon draped over the top of the gold frame. Wearing light tan pants and shirt and a sun hat, a woman was holding a trowel and leaning against a huge block of stone with others. "Is that...?"

"Yes, Irene Albertine, in happier times," he said without pause. "That picture is from the first trip I'd seen her. She stood out from the crowd a bit. Had a lot of answers to my questions. Time went on, and then our paths crossed here." He frowned. "It was a hard trip, that one, to open desert in the remote Valley of the Monkeys. A fierce sandstorm kicked up, and our group got lost in it. I almost didn't get out." He hesitated, "Some didn't."

Diane raised an eyebrow. "You mean...?"

"Things happen unexpectedly in the desert." He walked over to a spiny cactus and watered it. "And in life."

Diane said, "I guess so. Look what happened to Ms. Albertine. Which is why I wanted to meet with you. I'm hearing and seeing more about how accomplished she was, and had a passion for ancient Egyptian culture and art."

"She took after her father on that," Cedric said.

"Also, she could be somewhat intense, or difficult, even unfriendly."

"You mean intimidating, irritating," he said knowingly. "She didn't used to be."

Diane asked, "No? Have any ideas what brought about the change?"

Cedric sat behind his desk. "Her mother, Ava, died. They were close."

Diane wrote in her notebook: *Irene had a rough time accepting her mother's death.*

Cedric cleared his throat. "Before then, she resented what had happened to her mother. In a word, divorce. Max had walked away from Ava. That kicked off great unhappiness in her mother and Irene. But Irene still loved her dad. Right up to the end. An era has passed, my dear."

"Did he leave her for someone else?" As far as Diane knew, there was no current Mrs. Albertine, or a girlfriend. Philandering seemed unlikely, but worth the ask.

He raised his chin. "Common, but not so."

"Oh." That kind of reason for a divorce was most hurtful to the one left behind. Especially for children to cope with. Their dad didn't like their mom anymore? How could that be?

"Ava was very insecure, and they married young. Max's rejection drove her off her noggin." He tapped his temple. "She found solace in pints at a pub. She didn't make it home one night. Shock to all."

"Max had mentioned this," Diane said.

"Didn't help much that Max was in Egypt when it happened. He says that's when Irene became testy about everything. Never went back to the fun girl she once was. But I still liked her a lot. Her work was her life." He seemed tense when he said it, disappointed even. "We shared that much."

The sudden tap on Cedric's door made them both jump. He called for the visitor to come in. An adult male student, broad-shouldered and taller than he, in his thirties, stepped inside.

"Are you available to sign off on my last progress report?" He waved a yellow paper at Cedric.

Cedric glanced at Diane and back to him. "Hello, Peter. Can you come back, please?"

"I'd rather not."

Diane gazed at him. He did seem hurried and unable to stand still.

Cedric paused, then said, "Fine. Bring it here." He looked over the page and signed.

The student brushed past Diane and snatched the document away from his lab instructor.

Cedric said flatly. "Just be careful next time?"

Peter frowned. "It was an *accident,* is all. *Exam pressure,* you know? But thank you." His expression was agitated, his tone cool, defensive.

Diane pulled in her feet so Peter wouldn't trip over them as he left. The door banged shut.

"Excuse me." Cedric said into the silence. "That was Peter's ticket to get back in the good graces of the Stahlboard Foundation. He was put on probation here at Albertine's after he came back from a ten-day suspension back in July." He ran his fingers over his forehead. "I'm bloody hoping for no more issues with him, or like that. Handling them makes me wish I were out in the field near Saqqara."

Diane shook her head. "Whatever could he have done?"

Cedric said, "A fair question. In my lab, gloves are always worn while handling an artifact." He leaned back in his chair. "Peter Osborn was spotted without them during a dusting exam. Then, he bumped a canopic jar almost off the lab table."

Diane held back a gasp.

"Luckily, he caught it on the way to the floor." He shut his eyes for a few seconds and frowned. "Three thousand years almost laid in shards. I wanted to bloody thrash him." Cedric glared at the door with contempt. "I ran the situation through Academic Affairs. That'd be Max... and Peter's temporary suspension was suggested."

"I see."

"Two weeks later, Peter got a letter from Stahlboard about his change of status, and that he'd been bumped to the alternates list."

"So, he's lost his job placement chance?"

"Perhaps. We're in a new session now for fall. Peter's probation will be over in December. One more sloppy infraction, though, and he's out of here." Cedric laid another book on the pile with a heavy thud. "I'm sure that sounds tough. But you'd understand more than most how someone has to pay for their serious mistakes?"

Diane nodded. "We do what we have to do." Her deep-seated respect for rules and protocol made it easy for her to see Cedric's point. Rarely did she feel a tinge of sympathy for perpetrators during tormented confessions. Usually, their impaired judgment had justified a heinous act. To her, nothing justified murder.

"Anyway, Peter doesn't handle failure well. He came here fresh out of divorce, which he looked at as a failure. Stahlboard's reaction to his mistake rattled Peter. We've all been required to provide them progress reports. I sign off on his. Meanwhile, his working in the Nile Valley waits."

"What did he do during his suspension. Go home?"

"He kept his living quarters here, appealed his probation, and hung out at Millie's playing darts. Got quite good at it, I've heard."

Diane turned back to Irene. "So, Cedric, did Irene ever mention she was worried about trouble coming at her?"

"Do you mean like threats?"

"Or the like? Or anything disturbing to Mr. Albertine?"

"Not that I know."

Diane looked at the books on Cedric's desk. One of them was written by the victim.

"We have a ton of these on hand now," Cedric said. "Here, have one."

Diane accepted the copy. "I'm sure her loss is felt."

"Immensely so."

She opened it to the front pages and noted who was listed in the acknowledgments. She recognized none of the names, but they were important enough for Irene to list them. Her color photograph filled the back cover jacket. So fitting, it brought an inward smile to Diane. The victim was sitting atop a camel in front of an ancient tomb.

Cedric offered, "It's Nefertari's tomb. She was Ramesses II's wife. A most brilliant, exemplary tomb full of hieroglyphics and reliefs. The colors were preserved so well they look like they were used this morning." His eyes burned with excitement. "Have you been to Egypt, Mrs. Phipps?"

Diane regretted to say no, then, "What're your thoughts about what happened here?"

Cedric leaned in closer and gazed down at a pen. "For the record, I see you're doing your job. But I don't know who killed her."

As he looked up, Diane thanked him. "It's for me to figure out." She closed her notebook. "And I must get going. I'm eager to visit the crime scene."

"Ah, yes. The ballroom. I've not been in there since the Night of the Scarab event. See the Events Coordinator, Margaret Callaway, to let you in. Her office is next to the lobby."

"Thank you, and a pleasure." She rose from the chair as Cedric crossed the short space to his door and opened it. "I wish meeting you were under more pleasant circumstances."

"Likewise."

"We'll meet again," she said.

"Bravo."

Diane secured her purse strap over her shoulder and left "Professor Row" hallway with her first interview checked off her list. Learning about how Irene had reacted to her mother's divorce and death had been enlightening. The victim hadn't really moved on, which caused her to "close up" socially. Understandable, and treatable.

Seven

Tour of the Crime Scene

Minutes later, Diane introduced herself to Margaret, Event Assistant, and expressed her plan to visit the crime scene. "Certainly," Margaret said and pressed a button on her desk phone. "Ben, could you please escort Ms. Phipps to the Luxor?" She quickly sat down in her office chair. "Yes, she's here in my office. Thank you. No, I'll not be joining her. No, security isn't an issue. She's been invited by Mr. Albertine to investigate Irene's case. Thanks."

Margaret hung up and frowned. "I'm sorry to pass you along, but I'd rather not go in there. Ben's our room manager. He knows the room and lights, and how to operate the curtain. He can answer your questions about the space. Maximilian is on his way here now. He'll want to touch base with you. One more thing, perhaps you'd like a seating chart for that evening?"

"Yes, please. I'll stop by here before I go back to the Oasis to see Mr. Albertine."

Margaret handed her the paper. "You're in for a treat, Ms. Phipps. That room has been transformed into a replica from the burial chamber of Ramesses II. Much like what had happened in the original tomb, painstaking work went into our ballroom. The ballroom hasn't been touched for weeks except the artifacts on display have been removed and are on show in the museum. Other events scheduled for the ballroom have been cancelled."

Diane clutched her notebook. Her goal was still to pin down a motive, which historically had pointed to a murderer. But seeing where the death happened exposed the logistics, even the opportunity for committing murder. As unique as people's fingerprints, the Luxor Ballroom might be holding its own trove of clues. The space had a dreadful history, and Diane prepared to check things out in her own way.

~ * ~

Summoning her objectivity, Diane entered the room and felt the pall immediately. Ben turned on the lights, chandeliers, and showed her the switch that operated the curtain. "My extension is three-eight-four, if you should need something."

He left her alone for her walk-through. Diane waited for her eyes to adjust to the diminished light, and for the room to visually "talk" to her. Although the scene had been previously combed for evidence and clues, now was her chance to form her own impressions first-hand. Yellow crime tape lay in a pile near the door. Floral centerpieces still on the tables had dried.

Resolutely, Diane walked further into the Luxor Ballroom. Indeed, she stood in a replica tomb chamber of Ramesses II. Despite its magnificence, the stage stole her attention.

She stepped over to the curtain switch and flipped it on. Embossed with a gold scarab dead center, the red velvet curtain rose smoothly and noiselessly. Gazing at the relit stage, she wanted to think like one of the guests. But she'd better think like the killer, walk in his footsteps.

Diane wended her way through the disarray of tables and chairs and mounted the four steps on stage right. The black floorboards under her feet were lightly scraped or pitted. She recalled the stage set-up from the sheriff's photos she'd studied. The props used to hold the star of the show were still in place, along with those used to hold the coffin base and lid upright.

She walked to center stage and turned to face the open room and tables. Their cloths, some pulled askew, formed an irregular patchwork of red and blue. Many place settings no longer claimed their rightful space and various water glasses had tipped. Chairs had lost their places, and copies of Irene's book were left behind. It was an eerie tableau—with no people—all pointing to chaos. Exit doors, one left and one right, lead to side hallways. Possible escape routes for the killer?

Diane had never developed an interest in theatre or performing arts. Still, she mused, standing up there, one felt a certain kind of power. A certain kind of opportunity. Sure, it fed those hungry for applause. They used the stage as their refuge, their home. Establishing a connection with the audience made them work for encores that translated into acceptance.

But for Irene Albertine, there were no actors, no lines to memorize, no blocking to learn. She was killed on stage for real in act one at the hand of a merciless killer. The perp had stolen the show, a private show. No ticket needed. No witnesses watched, except for a forever silent, dried-up mummy.

The evidence previously collected came to Diane's mind. Scant grains of sand on the floor lay by the prop that held up Set-Nohr. Fibers. Where had the fibers come from? An old button with scratching on it. The white napkin murder weapon—how did he come by that? Had he eaten in the Sphinx Café? More questions bombarded her.

Why stuff the victim into the coffin? Why not drop the body down the trap door of the stage to hide it? Or simply lug Irene offstage and out the back door? Was time a factor? Had the killer spoken to her? What were his words?

Diane frowned. Sleepless nights of conjecture loomed in her direct future. Stumped, she pulled her cell phone from her pocket and captured images for her use. Time drifted into an hour of crime scene scrutiny, including under the stage. She recorded her findings. "Dim, low ceiling. Dusty concrete floor, no footprints. Space mostly empty except for boxes of flood lights, coils of sound wire, and an old empty wardrobe trunk. End."

She shut off the recording and left beneath the stage as a woman walked into the ballroom. Her tan Center knit shirt with a forest green logo embroidered on the front and long-legged jeans marked her as an employee.

"Excuse me," the woman called to her. "I'm sorry to interrupt."

Diane closed the low stage doors behind her and stepped out into the room. "I'm almost finished here, and—"

"I'm Katie Melrose, and I work in the museum gift shop." She dragged a wheeled metal cart behind her.

"Ahh, nice to meet you. Diane Phipps," she returned with some briskness. "Am here regarding Ms. Albertine's case."

Katie left the cart and came closer. "Sure, I've heard. But Mr. Roberts has asked me to clear the books from this room. He says they've been in here long enough. I'll try not to bother you."

"Mr. Roberts?" The name rang a bell from the sheriff's list of staff.

"He's my boss, the gift shop manager." She stepped to the nearest table and lifted one of the books. "Oh, good. They're not dusty," she said with relief. She appeared to be in her late twenties, a thin and wily frame, and had bright blue eyes. Her blond curly hair fought all sense of order. Her mission pushed her to the next table. "I'm to take all these copies of Irene's book back to the shop. Mr. Albertine wants us to set up a larger memorial display in her honor."

Diane repocketed her phone. "Would you like some help?"

Katie welcomed the offer. Diane turned and headed for the empty cart and pulled it closer to them. "So, you knew Irene?"

"Yes." Katie gathered a few books in her arms and dropped them on the top shelf of the cart with a thump.

Expecting more than a flat response and a thump, Diane waited.

Katie then said, "I'll speak for myself. She was a thorn in my side. So, there you have it."

Diane wasn't surprised. Accounts of Irene's dour social exchanges were mounting up. Now, here was another one. Diane was beginning to believe her father's comment that she had a short friend list. Still, surely Irene befriended at least a few folks. Maybe even someone loved her? That would be worth knowing more about. She tucked the thought away for further pursuit.

Meanwhile, Katie's pleasant expression faded.

"Do you care to share why?" Diane asked.

"She was critical. She never cared for my visual merchandising ideas. I'd spend hours on creating displays, which were approved by Mr. Roberts, and she'd come through and say, 'Try again, dear.'"

"Frustrating, at least."

Katie nodded her head repeatedly. "Frustrating to no end. Mr. Roberts would go round and round with her over pricing, or stocking kinds of popular artifact replicas. Like the famous Nefertiti bust statue. Irene really didn't want them in the gift shop. You know why?"

Diane replied, "Try me."

"Because Nefertiti has only one eye! The artifact was found that way in 1912, and nobody really knows why it was left unfinished. Irene, the great Egyptian art scholar, found it... *imperfect*. She and Mr. Roberts even raised their voices over stocking it."

"My goodness."

It was clear Katie was warming up. "One time, after she left, I heard him say, 'Wish we could get rid of her.'" As soon as the words left her mouth, Katie rolled her eyes. "Oh, no! I'm sure he didn't mean it like that... I mean, with what happened to her. So terrible."

Diane shared a silent beat with her. "Probably not," Diane finally said, but with reservation. The possibility that Mr. Roberts decided to get rid of Irene Albertine for good crossed her mind. Had their differences escalated to that point? Sadly, homicides happened for a lot less. Reading the sheriff's interview notes about Mr. Roberts tonight might offer her a new insight. For now, jumping to conclusions would get her nowhere.

Meanwhile, Diane collected more books and chatted with Katie—a bit of luck. Again, Diane was reminded how even reticent people opened up to her, which proved more helpful than not. She could use this time to learn more. Perhaps Katie had noticed other things.

She asked lightly, "Were there others with whom Irene had a strained relationship?"

Katie brushed hair away from her face after layering more books on the cart. "Sure. Maybe no one mentioned that

Louis Millard in graphics avoided her like the plague. Well, that didn't work much. But he had the same issues with her as me. They had a big row over the invitations for the Night of the Scarab Gala. Louis created a design because it was part of his job, and Irene, being Irene, designed one, too. Funny thing was, they both used a scarab on the invitation. Mr. Albertine stepped in to pick the one he liked best. He picked Irene's. Big surprise, right?"

Diane suppressed a smirk, as Katie whispered, "Louis's was better, just between you and me. Louis's a good artist. He designed the logo for the institute, after all. Anyway, it was Mr. Albertine's idea to use a red wax seal on the back of the envelope, which I thought was brilliant. Margaret suggested we put an invitation on display in the gift shop, and both Mr. Roberts and Mr. Albertine went for it." Katie batted her eyelashes as if flirting.

Diane caught her gist. Since it was handed to her, she asked, "So you think they have a thing for Margaret? Both of them?"

Katie answered, "Mr. Albertine is ahead in that race. Half the time he wears that red scarf Margaret gave him. And, one day I went into the back stockroom for a Nefertiti statue for a museum member, and Margaret was retying his tie for him."

"Hmm. I wonder—how did Irene feel about them?"

"Word around here is that she was perturbed. She liked things that were *her* idea. Margaret figured it was none of Irene's business."

Diane lodged the romantic connections in her mind and went on. "Did you happen to notice anything or anyone unusual the day of the gala?"

Katie raised her hands in a flurry. "Oh my, we were so busy. Many guests had checked in early and were milling about. We had a guest book table set up out in the corridor.

Mr. Roberts sent me in around six to add Irene's book to the lectern and a glass of water for Mr. Albertine for when he was to give his talk. I used one of the side doors, and Cedric was on his way out. He'd left a small gift for Max at his place setting. And a maintenance guy and a catering lady came out right after, too."

"Cedric?"

"Yes, he's English and is one of our visiting adjuncts, and an Egyptologist."

"We've met."

"Good friend of Mr. Albertine's. I'd asked him if he thought everything was ready. He scooted past me without a word, which kind of miffed me. But nothing seemed out of the ordinary, except the ballroom no longer looked like our Luxor Ballroom. Took a person's breath away."

Diane stepped closer. "Katie, can you remember if the curtain was up or down?"

"Sure. It was very down. It only took me about two minutes to put the things in place and leave. Gary, the photographer, was coming in the main doors just as I was leaving. He was dressed up and carrying all his camera stuff. I don't think he saw me, though."

Diane pressed further. "While you were in there, did you hear anything unusual?"

Katie replied. "Nothing. The music wasn't playing yet, so it was quiet as a tomb. Er, no disrespect meant." She crinkled her nose and placed the last books on the cart. "I should get back now. Mr. Roberts is waiting."

"Thank you," Diane said. Her impressions of behind-the-scenes life at the institute were growing by leaps and bounds. Nonetheless, she felt she was only getting started.

Remembering to stop by Margaret's office, she retraced the route. Sure enough, Mr. Albertine and she were amicably having coffee. They invited her to stay, but she declined.

"Sheriff Cotton texted me for updates," she explained. "And I'm ready to go back to my suite, which is lovely by the way, for reading more of his reports."

Max seemed pleased.

Eight

Visit With Caroline

Diane's evening brought more reading and notetaking. She also found a video of the crime scene and gave it another chance to tell her something she or the sheriff had missed. It included guests who were shuttled off to one area of the room until they could leave. The woman in a white caftan and beaded headpiece caught Diane's attention. She'd taken the trouble to wear Egyptian-style evening wear. Diane's curiosity burned, and she called Sheriff Cotton.

"She's Caroline Carver, a local donor to the museum and a friend of the victim."

A friend of Irene's? How close they were she'd yet to learn. "I'd like to meet her." Excitement fluttered through her. A true friend could reveal important things and even secrets they'd shared. They could have bearing on the case.

"Her contact info is listed on my interview report. She's reclusive, so good luck."

The next day Diane called Caroline and made tracks to her home. With searching for a motive still on her mind, she lifted the heavy brass door knocker (shaped like a sphinx) and let it drop loudly. Her second knock brought results, as Caroline opened the door herself.

She smiled slowly and stood back for Diane to enter. Silver gray hair framed her broad tanned face. She appeared to be in her sixties, and exuded poise.

"Thank you for calling," she said. She wore sand-colored jeans, boots with turquoise leather tassels, and a flame red shirt. Silver earrings topped off her attire. She had no trouble making eye contact with Diane.

"I'm here about Irene Albertine."

"Yes, of course." In another few minutes, Diane had followed her back to the posh music room. A white grand piano dominated the room, and Diane stood transfixed in awe. "Gorgeous," slipped from her mouth. "Do you play?"

"Come, sit here," Caroline said and indicated a comfy pale blue, overstuffed chair. "Yes, I play. Have for years—I'm classically and concert trained. But arthritis has changed all that." She lifted her hands for Diane to see the swelling of her joints.

"Painful?" Diane asked.

"Not usually, but stiffer than playing Rachmaninoff allows." She sank onto a wicker chair near a tea cart. "But you're here about Irene."

Diane handed her a card. "I'm told you were friends."

"It's true. We met three years ago through the Osiris Society. I'm missing her terribly," she said solemnly. "And Max and Cedric must be going nuts."

Diane opened her little notebook. "They're trying to get used to it, too, I guess."

Caroline huffed, "Lord, who gets used to murder?"

Diane inwardly gave her points for that. "I'm sure they have their moments, dealing with her loss and mourning. I'm wondering about her funeral."

"I went. Her funeral was... dismal," Caroline said. "Over at Sweeney's Funeral Home. It was private as private gets; three days after she died. No guest book to sign. Closed casket and flowers on top. I managed to play 'Amazing Grace' on their out-of-tune piano. Coffee and cookies directly after Rev. Bishop finished. No gravesite service."

Diane wrote quickly, and said, "Still emotional for some."

Caroline added, "Low attendance. Some paid their respects out of social or work obligations. Most remained dry-eyed as a potato. Some really came for Max, who was broken up. Margaret sat with him. I sat with Cedric. Very distraught."

"Was anybody missing? I mean, they should've come, but didn't?"

Caroline shrugged. "It's beyond me, but I *liked* Irene. She was unusual. A perfectionist; disagreeable at times. Knew her stuff, too. She didn't ask anyone to do anything she wouldn't have done. She liked fashion, too, but wasn't very good at putting outfits together. We planned to wear our caftans to the gala. Irene's was purple, and she had an amazing collar to go with it like an Egyptian queen would've worn." Caroline took in a breath and let it out in a gush. "Irene was also a button collector, and she didn't even sew. She found art in everything." She closed her eyes for a moment. "She just had high expectations is all."

Diane felt her pain. "Some folks are just misunderstood, even feared."

"I certainly wasn't afraid."

"You managed well with her. So, tell me about Irene and Cedric Hardwick."

Caroline's eyes brightened. "That man was in love with her. They first met in Egypt; she went on a field trip and they got lost in a sandstorm. They made it out alive, but their guide didn't."

Diane's interest soared. "My goodness." She was no archaeologist, but her heart skipped a beat. Archaeologists were kindred spirits in a way because they were also detectives. They sifted through material evidence that revealed how people lived in ancient Egypt, which was of great interest, not to mention the value of any artifacts uncovered.

Caroline looked up at the ceiling, recalling a moment. "Bothered the heck out of Irene that one of Nefertiti's eyes was missing; ruined the whole statue."

"Joking, right?"

"No. Irene liked ancient things, but in good condition. 'Better resale value,' she'd once said. Personally, I thought the no left eye thing made the relic more authentic. Her sculptor didn't finish their job, which irritated Irene. But I didn't say anything. She didn't like people disagreeing with her, and I like keeping the peace, so..." Caroline uncrossed her legs and stood. "Would you like tea?"

Diane accepted the offer. "Sugar, no cream, please." More sides of the victim were surfacing. Rather undesirable traits. Yet, Cedric had fallen in love with her.

"Do you know of any other friends Irene might've had in the area?"

Caroline served her cup of tea on a small silver tray. "Maybe a few. She had kind things to say about Dr. Granbury and a couple of students. She liked museum donors, and we supported her work."

"Her work?"

"Sure. She still went to Cairo; came home with artifacts for the museum. Even for private purchase. She'd just returned from a trip in time for the gala and her father's birthday." Carolyn smiled wistfully. "She'd even reserved her favorite camel, Chester, for the trip. Imagine that.'"

Diane drank tea. "Chester the camel?"

"Chester, indeed. She would hit the desert with him. From what I gathered, she rode around and looked at... sand, I suppose. And ate dates, slept in a tent under the stars."

Diane could think of better vacations. "Alone?"

Caroline looked ceilingward. "She'd mentioned Javier, a good guide. He reserved Chester for her. Javier knew back routes, where water was, and he knew a lot of diggers, which made her happy. She loved going. There was no one around to deny her whims."

Diane drank all this in, along with her tea when her phone dinged. Incoming message from Sheriff Cotton. *Come to my office.*

She soon replied, *On my way.*

Nine

Set-Nohr Arrival

Diane arrived at Sheriff Cotton's office at 3:10 p.m. Just in time to hear Buck Dawson give his report.

"Good afternoon, Ms. Phipps," Buck said. "Are things going well?"

Diane sat next to him. "I'm learning more, but I don't have a suspect yet. How's it going with apprehending those two fugitives who most likely didn't pilfer Irene Albertine's necklace?"

Buck swung his head toward her.

"Never mind," Sheriff Cotton cut in. "Go on, Buck. Let's hear what you've got."

Buck leaned forward and rested his elbows on his knees. "She's right."

Diane swallowed and held his gaze.

Sheriff Cotton slapped his desktop with his hand. "How do you know that?"

"Raphael and his girl were in Albuquerque the night of Albertine's murder."

"Confirmed?" Diane asked, trying not to shout 'Yay!'

"They were caught red-handed at a big casino party soiree. Lotta jewels, lotta cash. Lotta opportunity. They were apprehended... and they skipped during transport."

Sheriff Cotton's eyes bugged. "They got away?"

Dawson repeated, "Away. But I'm sticking here. Raphael's cousin lives a few miles outside of Alamosa."

"Want us to put a spotter on him?" the sheriff asked.

"Might help, but it looks like he's not a kissin' cousin. He's agreed to cooperate with us if, or when, they show up."

"Smart. Aiding and abetting will get him two to six years," Diane said.

Dawson gave her a nod. "I'm thinking Raphael will make a pit stop there on their way to his next gig."

Diane shook her head. Incredible how well people pull off being on the lam. She gave Dawson an appreciative look. Truthfully, he looked a little peaked. His jacket hung on the back of the chair, white shirt unbuttoned at the top, and his black tie loosened.

"I hope you're right," she said.

Sheriff Cotton swiped his eyebrow and let out a couple of cuss words. He shifted his gaze to Diane. "And what do you have? Update, please."

She opened her notebook. "Several things. Irene Albertine had a whole passel of people not liking her. She turned sour after Mr. Albertine divorced her mother, Ava, who took to the bottle and crashed her car."

"We have that on record," Sheriff Cotton noted.

"Now it's on mine too," she tapped her notebook. "Here's more. Cedric Hardwick was in love with Irene. Caroline Carver, friend, says Irene wasn't cranky. She just had high standards, and she had a little thing going on the side."

Sheriff Cotton's eyes flickered with interest. "A thing?"

"She collected buttons."

Unimpressed, he said, "So did my grandmother. Go on."

"Irene's funeral was private, and few people cried."

"I noticed," he said.

"Katie Melrose, gift shop, ran into Cedric and a couple other staffers coming and leaving the ballroom an hour before the event, including the photographer, name unknown, walked in the main door with his photo gear."

"His name is Randy McPherson," Sheriff Cotton added.

Diane jotted it down. "Katie reports nothing seemed out of place or wrong. The red curtain was down. She and her boss, Mr. Roberts, had little regard for Irene. They spat with her about items stocked in the shop. Same with Louis in graphics. Big fight erupted with Irene over the invitations for the Night of the Scarab Gala."

"A regular sweetheart," Buck said.

"There's more. Cedric would really rather be working out in the field; he ran into an issue with a student named Peter Oborn over a lab procedure, and Peter was suspended for a while. He's still here, on probation. Mr. Albertine does have a girlfriend, Margaret Calloway, the event assistant. Irene wasn't happy about it. The victim had continued her Cairo trips and had returned to Albertine's the day before the gala. She planned to return to Egypt shortly after the event."

"She never slowed down," Cotton noted.

"Irene must've been tough... she got out of a sandstorm alive during a field trip to the Valley of the Monkeys some years back. Cedric had organized the trip. Margaret supplied me with the gala seating chart for the dinner. My visit to the Luxor Ballroom produced nothing new, except more questions. Good job, Sheriff."

Buck Dawson ran his hand down his jaw. "How long you been doing this?"

"Several years--long enough to trust my eyes and hunches."

Sheriff Cotton's frown faded as he raised his hands. "What's next?"

"Tomorrow, I want to visit the victim's residence."

~ * ~

Diane left the sheriff's office and lunched at Millie's. Her afternoon free from interviews, she drove to the Albertine Egyptian Museum. One-story and round, the building stood adjacent to the Institute and was wrapped in sand-colored brick. Undoubtedly, it was an Albertine Architecture contemporary design, with high-up windows to preserve interior wall space for displays.

She parked in the lot and approached the automatic glass front door, which was etched with a pyramid. One tap on a gold plate mounted on the brick caused the door to open for her. She'd visited more than her share of museums through the years, and stepping into this one told her she was about to tour a unique one. Two men worked behind a tall welcome desk. While one spoke on the phone, the other waved at her and smiled. She approached him and paid the entry fee. His nametag read Edward Miller, Archivist. He handed her a brochure with a museum map inside. A good thing, as it was spacious with many rooms.

"Welcome, ma'am. Having a pleasant day?" he asked.

"Good so far, thanks." She had much to mull through on this new case, especially with jewel thieves out of the picture. But coming here would give her mind a break and help her familiarize herself with more of the victim's world.

"You may enjoy," Edward began, "our Set-Nohr mummy video in the Lotus Courtyard. The film features our late Irene Albertine with her father on the arrival of Set-Nohr. The mummy is currently off-exhibit, but the film shows wonderful details of her."

Diane appreciated the tip and wandered a bit. Eventually, she stopped in the Lotus Courtyard. Washed in daylight and covered with a glass ceiling, indirect lighting warmed the small alcoves in three corners. The fourth was set up as a small theater with three rows of padded benches for seating. She ambled over to a tall obelisk engraved with Egyptian art. An olive tree stood next to the fountain where gold snakes spouted water into the middle. Large blue Lapis urns were filled with lofty, water-loving papyrus and lotus plants. They caught wayward splashes from the fountain. She settled on a bench in the video alcove while the film played.

She watched intently. A large truck rolls up to the back of the warehouse building. The driver and his helper are greeted by Edward, Maximilian, Cedric, and Irene. All are smiling. The drivers open the back door of the truck. Edward brings over the mobile scissor lift standing by to meet the edge. All the men push the huge wooden box onto the lift.

Done, they all cheer, and Irene claps with glee as they roll it into the building. After moving the mummy transport crate into a large work area, they stop for a breath. Edward brings an electric screwdriver to open the shipping crate. There's much anticipation and chatter. The lid is removed, layers of packing excelsior are removed, and everyone stands still with reverence and gapes. Maximilian hugs his daughter.

Diane wanted to cheer with them. It was almost like Christmas.

The rest of the shipping crate is broken away and falls with a clatter. Holding a clipboard, Irene writes. Lighting is turned up. Cedric and Maximillian discuss the fine quality of the painting and inscriptions on the coffin surfaces. Cedric translates the hieroglyphics aloud.

Diane was awed with his ease of doing so and watched more.

Randy, photographer/videographer, captures close-ups of the details. Excitement builds, and the crew carefully removes the top lid of the coffin. Set-Nohr's face mask and linen wrapped body are wholly exposed. Fresh air meets ancient surfaces. Set-Nohr is now free, in her forever mummy form.

The crew carries the lid to another table and quickly returns to gaze upon their prize. Irene presents champagne and glasses, and Maximilian pops the cork. Cedric ignores the camera and kisses her on the mouth. Irene pulls away. Maximilian and Edward laugh, and they all toast their new acquisition. The screen goes dark.

Diane sat alone in the dim light and drifted into thought. Watching this, it was difficult to believe that two weeks later Irene was dead. Who in the world had suddenly popped their cork enough to murder her? Or was this a case of long-term planning?

Diane still had a lot of ground to cover. She needed to dig more into Irene's personal life.

Cedric was part of it. Caroline had told her he wanted to marry Irene, but she refused. It seemed a long shot, but more than once a spurned lover couldn't handle rejection and paid it back through homicide. Had Cedric broken down? She called him for an appointment.

"Would like to meet up," he said, "but I'm booked all day, and have a staff dinner tonight. Max wants to discuss how to proceed with re-opening the ballroom. He's found a chariot he might add to the museum."

"Sure, understandable. How about the day after tomorrow?"

"Certainly, at ten?"

Diane agreed and penned it in her notebook.

Tomorrow, however, she would visit Irene's apartment. Looking for clues might take hours. But what better way for Diane to spend her billable time on the job? Max deserved accurate updates on who killed his daughter. Diane hoped to tell him soon who done it and why.

Ten

Trouble at Irene's Apartment

Walking into Irene Albertine's large apartment, Diane wasn't sure for what she was looking. Just after dawn, she had recharged her cell phone for recording and snapping pics. Overall, she hoped for more answers than questions. Irene had lived on the top floor of a separate, two-story building for staff living. Using a shot-gun approach, she began with a wide sweep of the five rooms. She made a rough floor plan in her notebook. Little surprise, the rooms were all well-appointed.

It seemed incongruous to Diane that for perfectionist Irene, her living quarters were cluttered. Pile management in many cases, which made Diane's search work more of a chore. In some areas, it looked like someone had gone through Irene's things. Was this a new development, or had she missed something in Sheriff Cotton's notes?

For sure, a post-funeral disposition of her belongings hadn't been done. It would've been for Mr. Albertine to initiate that. But more than two months had passed. Perhaps it was still too soon for him, or for him to delegate the job to someone else? Either way, Irene's material life was bountiful.

Diane removed her windbreaker and hung it over the knob of the guest closet in the entryway. She set her tote bag and Thermos full of coffee on the entryway table and walked into the living room.

It was unabashedly quiet, and the morning sun poured through the long picture window. Again, Diane could see the dunes. If she used the binoculars sitting on the sill, she would see way deeper into the sand field. The back of the curved sectional sofa and the coffee table were awash with sunlight.

Disheveled as things were, Diane saw no dust. Irene's cleaning service must still be in respectful service. She pressed forth, exploring the rest of the rooms. Irene's office came next.

She crossed the hardwood floor to the large pedestal desk with its front legs carved into tall skinny cats, commemorating those the Egyptians had worshipped. Oil lamps were set about for accent light. In contrast to the rest of the room, the desk was completely clean and organized.

A small statue of Ramesses II claimed one corner. Nefertari's image rested next to Ramesses II. A funerary shabti mounted on a thick chunk of gold served as a paperweight. Irene's laptop and cell phone lay centered in front of the cream leather desk chair. They'd made a trip to the sheriff's office for scrutiny and had been returned. No threats were found on either.

Diane sat in Irene's chair and opened desk drawers on both sides. A plump bright blue fountain pen in one caught her eye, and she picked it up to admire. She opened her notebook to give it a try on a fresh page. Uncapping the pen, she expected to find the gold pen point. But she found none. She peered into the cavity and spotted a piece of paper rolled up like a scroll.

She carefully pried the slip of paper out with a paperclip and unfurled it in her palm. Numbers had been written on it: 32 48 16.

Diane squinted at them. Had Irene hidden the numbers to a combination lock, or a safe? If so, where was it, and what was inside? Diane sighed. Finding a key to a safe deposit box instead might yield more answers or clues. She snapped a photo of the paper and tucked it back into the fancy blue cylinder.

Leaving the office, Diane next opened the door to Irene's bedroom. Her bed was perfectly made, supporting her tough perfectionist style. Apparently, she liked stuffed bears. Three of them sat upright against the bed pillows. Two rested on a bedroom chair. One helped hold books upright on a shelf.

"So, Irene had a whimsical side," Diane murmured with a smile.

Irene's closet became Diane's next search target. Her large walk-in with two rooms inside were filled with clothing, shoes, and jewelry. The overhead light came on automatically. A purple caftan hung on a velvet hanger on a wall hook. Caroline's mention of Irene wearing of this frock to the gala came to Diane's mind.

She shifted her attention from the caftan to a multi-strand bejeweled collar. It had been laid next to a jewel cabinet on a broad shelf. Irene would've turned heads at the gala with all this finery. But she never got the chance.

Diane opened the doors to the carved cabinet and gasped. Gold and gemmed jewelry flickered in the soft light. Earrings, Egyptian cuffs, necklaces, and rings galore. She peered closer, not daring to touch any of them.

A large gold cartouche hung on its fine chain from its own dainty hook. Her heart thumped. In the center rested a large, sinfully red gem... the rare red diamond? Was this

Irene's missing cartouche? How had it ended up back in Irene's closet? Or had it ever left?

Another idea struck Diane. Had the diamond in Irene's signature million-dollar-plus necklace been paste? It seemed plausible she wore a fake since she wore the necklace everywhere much of the time. Diane suddenly smiled wryly. Whoever swiped the necklace from Irene's dead body was walking around with a fine fake. Karma lived.

Better yet, it would seem that whoever had the fake in their possession was at the murder scene. Find the necklace, find the killer? Then she'd pack up and go home. But Diane had learned long ago that things were rarely as they seemed. Thus, her to do list just grew.

She needed to: Find the person with the necklace. Rationale: He or she would have to explain their presence at the murder scene.

Thinking on that, she shook her head. Snatching anything cold-heartedly from a dying or dead person labeled them as despicable, a criminal... or desperate? Not reporting the murder or calling for help further supported their desire to get away undetected. Which jewel thieves would do.

Secondly, she needed to identify the killer who wielded a chloroform-soaked white napkin lifted from the Sphinx Café, and to prove the killer and the thief were the *same* person. Double crime. Homicide and grand theft. Voila! Case closed: she could pack her bag and go home.

Diane's fingers tingled as she drew her cell phone from her pocket for documenting the cartouche with a photo. Finished, she admired all the shoes. Bam! The closet door slammed behind her and cut off the light. She tapped her phone for light and stepped to the door. Trying the handle proved useless. "Hello," she called out. "Hello? Who's out there?"

Silence answered.

She pounded on the wood. "Open the door!"

Silence. Punching in Sheriff Cotton's number, she waited. Voicemail answered for him. "Sheriff, I might've found Irene Albertine's stolen red diamond necklace," she said, her voice wavering.

Urgency pushed her to text him as well. No reply. She called the main desk at the Center and identified herself and her predicament. Her pulse thumped faster. She never much liked closed, dark places. Especially if she hadn't walked willingly into one like this.

Frustration soon followed. "Who puts a lock on a closet?" she muttered, then rolled her eyes. Yet, this was no ordinary closet. There had to be untold value in here. Still, she wanted out. She raised her foot and swift-kicked the shiny brass handle. It merely flopped up and down. A slow ten minutes crawled by until she heard voices and saw the light of day shining on Security Chief DiNardo and a maintenance guy.

~ * ~

An hour later, Sheriff Cotton was all serious ears, and collected pertinent details from her in his office.

"Who has keys to Irene's apartment?" Diane asked, hoping for a list.

"Your guess is as good as mine. It was her personal residence, not a hotel room."

Even so, she said, "I'll check with Margaret. She may have ordered extra keys for Irene."

Sheriff Cotton gave her an apprising look. "You okay?"

Diane almost grinned. "Worse has happened." She thought for a few seconds. "For the record, I'm not so sure this was an accident, like the cleaning lady or a maid finding the door open and closing it."

He paused, then, "You think somebody is getting nervous?"

"Hmm. Too early to know."

Sheriff Cotton folded his arms. "Somebody here?"

"Very here."

He raised eyebrows. "Not somebody who came to the gala, did the deed, and left?"

"Here," she repeated. "The incident could be a fluke, but I sense I've been warned. Somebody could want me out of here."

Sheriff Cotton's expression turned grave. "Warnings have a way of repeating themselves. D'you have a firearm with you?"

Diane closed her notebook. "Certainly. Pearl comes with me on my cases."

"Here's hoping you don't have to use her."

"Fortunately, I never have. Anything else?"

"Yes. Sarah Fremont is back in town. She was Irene Albertine's personal assistant."

Diane straightened. "Personal assistant? I noticed her name in a report but saw no notes. Had she not been interviewed?"

"Sarah left for Montana a week before Irene's death. She's due in here to see me next week."

Diane asked, "What took her to Montana?"

"Her father. Ailing health. He's passed, and she's come back to stay."

Diane scooted forward on the chair. "Mind if I meet with her?"

"Not at all." He looked relieved. "And you may want to meet Dr. Andrew Granbury. A paleontologist. He's a guest lecturer at the Center when he's available. He came to the victim's funeral and laid a pink lotus flower on the lid of the casket, kissed it, and left."

"A lotus?"

"Means enlightenment. Albertine told me what it was. I think Andrew copped it from the Lotus Courtyard at the museum. He and Irene used to sit in there and eat their lunches."

Diane let it pass. Despite that, Dr. Granbury didn't stay for the services at Irene's funeral, his actions still told her he thought a lot of her. "I look forward to meeting him." The more she could find out about Irene, the better chances she had solving this case.

Sheriff Cotton provided her with contact information for both. "By the way, Albertine would've been here with us this morning, but he's out on the dunes with his pal Cedric. He asks you to contact him."

"Another question. When the deputies searched Irene's apartment after her death, why didn't they find the necklace?" She was pressing the issue and knew it. Some search teams were better than others.

"I figure it wasn't there."

Diane let that sink in. "But it is now. Or maybe it was an oversight? That closet was loaded."

Sheriff Cotton sighed. "Perhaps. They looked for threats, notes on paper, to do lists, the usual. Drugs. Piles of cash. An empty safe. Financial mail. Other people's clothes." He winked at her. "Something weird, like lampshades made from human skin."

She smirked and moved on. "Have you told Mr. Albertine about me finding the necklace?"

"Certainly. He wants to know more."

"How about Buck Dawson?"

Sheriff Cotton's phone beeped. He answered, listened, and hung up. "He wasn't on the search team, and he's after fugitives, not personal effects. But it'd be a key tip for him. I'll let him know." He reached for his hat. "We're going to

Millie's on Friday night for some grub and music. Want to join us?"

Diane half shrugged. "Maybe." Thinking about it later, she figured she could use a relaxing night. Most of her interaction with folks since she'd been there was about work. Also, since Millie's was the social crossroads of Sandy River, somebody or something interesting might turn up about Irene. Only one way to find out.

Eleven

Lunch with Max and Mysterious Numbers

Lunch with Mr. Albertine at the Sphinx Café followed her visit with Sheriff Cotton. Her host and client unfolded his napkin with a snap and dropped it on his knee. His dress shirt, a blue, finely woven plaid, contrasted with the red scarf Margaret had given him. His hair was neatly combed, despite he'd just come in from the dunes. Which, to her, showed elements of respect and being a gentleman. It also revealed he was recovering from Irene's death, as he was paying attention to grooming. People in shock often neglected their appearance.

Diane didn't feel like she'd torment him with her questions or cause emotional outbursts common from the bereaved. Her work and probing could be harsh. But she'd learned that approaching things in a less confronting way took her further. Secrets were often revealed. In this case, however, Maximilian was her client and was paying her to ask questions... everywhere.

"Have any leads?" he asked her directly. So much for easing into things.

Diane set down her water glass and answered, "Not yet."

He considered that for a moment. "And you were locked in Irene's closet?"

"Yes."

"Hell." He frowned briefly and looked at the menu. "The special today is salmon. Interested?"

"Very," she said and picked rice pilaf and broccoli for the sides. "You've had more time to think, so again, who might've killed your daughter."

He shook his head. "Nothing new. I've been thinking about this since the day she died. But I can't put it together. I mean, you give me a problem about designing a building that breathes better, or even defies gravity, and I can give it to you. But this? This has me completely stumped."

Diane felt his frustration. "Just a different kind of a puzzle is all.'

That seemed to appease him. "So, you think you've found Irene's red diamond cartouche?"

"In her closet." She helped herself to a lemon slice from a thin white plate and dropped it in her water.

Puzzlement wrinkled his brow. "Where you were locked in?"

"The same, yes. Her bedroom closet." Unfolding her napkin, she stopped mid-turn. Instead of plain white, it was wine red with a meek fringe and the signature sphinx stitched on a corner. "Could you tell me more about the cartouche?"

Maximilian rubbed his forehead. "Her necklace was a gift from me. I'd bought it from a merchant in Memphis, Egypt during the trip when Irene's mother passed. I thought it would give Irene comfort. Must've worked because she wore it all the time."

Diane issued a comforting nod. "Was it insured?"

"Of course. Lloyds of London covers all of our assets, including the museum."

She commended him inwardly. "Were there two cartouches?"

"Two? Hardly not. Not two genuine ones, anyway. But Sarah would know better than I. She and Irene got along well. Sarah helped Irene with many things. Trip itineraries, her calendar, what to wear where--right down to that lotus sweatshirt she had. It wouldn't surprise me that a fake was ordered... just for safety." He added, "They probably shared girl things I'll never know about."

Diane hoped so. "I plan to meet with her, Mr. Albertine, and—"

"Maximilian, please?"

Diane acquiesced. "As you wish." She picked up her napkin from her lap. "Ahh. You've changed the café napkins."

Maximilian adjusted the cuff on his shirt. "Margaret suggested we do it as part of the upgrades for the gala. I agreed. The old white reminded me that one of our napkins was used as a murder weapon." His eyes flashed with disgust.

Diane got that hands down. "This new red is very nice."

"Right," he said dourly.

"When were they changed?" she asked.

"Three days before the gala."

"So, the killer was around here before that change."

Maximilian straightened his spine. "How much around?"

"Hard to say."

"Here, in the café?" he pressed.

"Which also put the person in very close vicinity of her."

"And the rest of us," he said ruefully.

Diane crossed her legs. "He knew his target. He was waiting for the right moment."

Maximilian grimaced and pushed out his lower lip. "Pre-meditated."

"Seems so."

"That's very disturbing." He checked his phone and looked back at her. "Curious. How do you know her killer was a man?"

Diane offered, "Muscle power and time suggest her attacker was male. First, it takes extra strength to control a struggling victim—"

"She certainly would've fought," he interjected. "She wasn't a quitter."

"—And held her still long enough for chloroform to do its job. Secondly, most women can't pick up a dead body and lay it in a coffin. Lastly, the coffin lid was picked up, carried about five feet, and put back on the bottom. This all had to happen quickly." She sipped some water. "Yes. I figure a guy pulled this off."

Maximilian tapped his temple. "Reasonable deduction."

"The sheriff likes it."

"No fingerprints?"

"None. Gloves came in handy."

~ * ~

The next day Diane got up early and was able to reach Tom, first by text, then with a call. His voice always fueled her, supported her, grounded her in her work.

"How's it going, dear?" he asked quickly.

"A dead body fell out of a mummy's coffin, for starters. Then, I think I found a missing necklace... belonged to the victim; it was gone from her body when found. The victim had a track record for stepping on people's toes."

"Short friends list?"

"Very."

"Bigger suspect list." From Tom's breathing, she could tell he was walking outdoors. Wind whistled around his words. "Any leads, persons of interest?"

"None yet, but there's a perp here somewhere. How about you?"

"Watch yourself."

"Absolutely. Just getting to know the possibilities. These folks eat Egyptology for breakfast, lunch, and dinner. I like the art. How about you? How's it going?"

"Intense. Two deaths. Both kids," he said. "I'll be here for a while."

Diane shuddered. Things got dangerous on the job for her, but things got outrageous for Tom. More than once, he came home injured. "Comes with the territory," he'd remind her if she raised a fuss.

"Do good," she said, as if she had to.

"No other way, baby."

She smiled. "One other thing. I found a series of numbers on a piece of paper stuffed inside a pen. Hidden on purpose. 32, 48, 16. Might be for a safe, am not sure."

Tom stalled for a moment. "Keep them in mind. She hid them for a reason."

"Will do. My intuition says they fit into this case."

"You're probably right." He paused. "Crap. I've gotta run. Love."

"Love you." Diane was unsure whether her sentiment made it to his ear before the call cut-off. But she again felt heartened for her work, and called Sarah Fremont, who agreed to meet her in an hour in the lobby at the Oasis Guest Inn. Not knowing what she looked like, Diane asked her what she'd be wearing. "My usual red hair," came the reply.

It wasn't a wig. Sarah rushed in and towered over her by four inches, at least. Her long, curly flaming red hair rivaled the red poppies Diane's grandmother used to grow. Purple shirt, purple bag, purple shoes and skinny jeans, and a big amethyst ring. Her fifty or so years defied fashion conventions for her age. She pulled it off with contrasting colors, bracelets, and... charm.

Diane introduced herself and gave her a card.

"I'd give you my card," Sarah said, "but I lost my job because I lost my boss."

"That's why I'm here," Diane said, as they walked toward the door leading to the outdoor swimming pool. "To help find out who caused this and why."

"Won't matter," Sarah muttered. "Irene is gone, but I have time on my hands. So, what would you like to know?"

Diane replied, "First, justice matters."

Sarah consented, "I'm hoping to see some soon."

They passed the pool and cabana, then hung a hard right. A horse stable and a moderate corral stood beyond. Three horses of different colors slowly approached them on the other side of the rough-hewn fence. She and Sarah stopped and lingered. "I just learned you were Irene's personal assistant."

"I was. I was away. I missed her funeral."

Diane remarked, "Unfortunate timing." She wanted to know how personal Sarah's work was to Irene. Had she shopped for groceries, cooked for her, drawn her bath?

"I helped Irene with all kinds of things. Correspon-dence, trip arrangements, and sometimes fashion tips. I made dinner reservations for her and Dr. Granbury. I put together trip itineraries for her, picked up her mail, made her tea, drove her around when she didn't feel like it. You name it."

"Can tell me more about her apparel and accessories? Specifically, her red diamond cartouche. It went missing."

They walked about twenty feet, and Sarah climbed the fence and perched on the top rail. Her mouth tightened. "It did? Which one? The fake, or the authentic one?"

Diane joined her with her bottom half hanging over the back and her feet locked onto the next rail down. "Ahh, so there are two." Their vantage point gave her a wide view of Mount Blanca. Snow had come early and already painted the peak white.

"Indeed. I suggested she have one made because she wanted to wear it everywhere. Astronomical value. Way risky to wear out and about. I was grateful she saw the sense in the idea." She rested her hands on the wood either side of her for balance. "I pray the real one wasn't taken."

"I found one in her closet," Diane said and balanced herself the same way. "Now, I'm not sure which one."

Sarah nodded. "Where is it?"

"With Sheriff Cotton. The real necklace whereabouts counts. Grand theft charges would be added. Snatching from a dead body was an easy theft."

Sarah frowned. "That's why someone killed her?"

Diane hesitated. Discussing motives with those close to the victim was questionable. But Sarah's eyes spilled disbelief and understandable concern. "I believe not, but the jury is still out on that."

"I hope not for long. It feels tense around here." She lowered herself off the fence with ease. "Anything else you'd like to know?"

Diane hopped down to the ground with a bump. "I'm wondering about Irene's friendship with Dr. Granbury."

"Ohhh, that," Sarah said and began walking along the fence line. "Irene was crazy about Andrew. Few knew of it because she preferred privacy."

This new twist in Irene's romantic life tantalized Diane's inquisitiveness. "So, Cedric wasn't her choice?"

The corner of Sarah's mouth lifted. "He was sort of, until Andrew arrived. Mind you, there really was a connection between Cedric and Irene. But it wasn't deep enough for Irene. Took a while for Cedric to catch on."

Diane matched Sarah's pace as they trudged over uneven ground and through the prairie grass. "She jilted him?"

"Not harshly; they had a lot in common with Egyptology and were devoted to Max's efforts here. Not long before she died, Cedric had proposed to her, and she didn't accept. I'd admired her for staying true to herself. Holding out for a better match."

"How'd Cedric take it?"

Sarah cut around a large tumbleweed caught in the fence and Diane followed.

"Max would know better than me," Sarah added. "They're good buddies. But I think Cedric threw himself into his work instead of moping over losing Irene." She stopped and mused aloud. "Amazing how a man's work can save him, isn't it? Cedric had a lot to do. Before Irene died, he was planning a project that would take him back to Egypt. He'd even approached Max about investing, but Max declined the offer. Then Cedric found what he needed from other sources. He would've been gone for two years."

"Sounds major."

"Probably an excavation," Sarah said. "Irene explained to me one time that a lot goes into launching an excavation, and money, too. Had to be of major interest for Cedric to put everything in motion. He needed sponsors, permissions, and on-site diggers lined up."

Diane listened as they headed back toward the swimming pool. These people's worlds were so different from hers.

"Anyway, Irene and Andrew were planning their own getaway. Andrew had requested a leave for after Thanksgiving. Irene hadn't said much to anyone about it, but she shared with me they would be gone for about a month, and I could take the time off. With pay."

"Generous of her."

"She could be. She was very excited about their trip." Sarah leaned down, picked up a greenish rock, gazed at it, and tossed it aside. "To tell you the truth, I thought she and Andrew were eloping. She asked me to get a bottle of Dom Perignon, her favorite champagne, to take with them. Have you met Dr. Granbury yet in your enquiries?"

Diane answered, "I will very soon."

Twelve

Fake or Real? and Dr. Granbury

Friday night rolled around fast, and Diane joined Sheriff Cotton and Buck Dawson at Millie's. They settled in a booth along the wall near the side door. From there, Diane could see the band and part of Dart Alley. Tables had been rearranged for a small dance floor.

Food ordered, Diane kicked back and watched folks dancing and the darts competition. But the case never really left her mind. Her knowledge and impressions about Irene had tripled, especially the part about her interest in Dr. Granbury.

Also, Cedric's project stirred Diane's curiosity. Perhaps, because she was becoming immersed in what archaeologists were uncovering to share with the world. Besides, some secrecy seemed to surround the nature of Cedric's project. Secrecy always beckoned her to uncover its core.

But maybe discretion was customary in archaeology until a project was fully in progress? Certainly, though, Cedric would've shared his intent with Maximilian. How about with Irene? Since Cedric had apparently abandoned his plans not long before Irene died, it probably was a moot point to learn more. Except, she found the timing interesting.

And on another note, had Irene and Dr. Granbury really planned to elope? More perplexing questions leap-frogged in her mind. Her time with Sarah Fremont proved to be fruitful, giving more fodder to sort through for pinpointing a perp. For now, she tapped her foot on the wood floor while the band covered "Mustang Sally."

Buck Dawson nudged her arm with his elbow. "I heard you went sightseeing and spent some time in a closet," he said, raising his voice a tad over the music.

She confirmed the incident with, "There were two necklaces."

He did a doubletake. "Confirmed?"

"To be determined which one is at the sheriff's office. Fifty-fifty chance the thief has the fake."

He took a draw on his draft beer. "My heart bleeds for the thief," he said with sarcasm.

"Mine for the murderer."

"Got a grip on that yet?"

Diane reached for some popcorn out of the basket on the table. "Victim had a lover. Her personal assistant figured they were going to elope." She began to munch. "Curious, isn't it? No reason to run away to get married. No family drama. No pressure I can see. No health issues. Weird."

"My grandparents eloped," Buck said out of the corner of his mouth. "My aunt said passion got away with them. My father arrived six months later."

Diane glanced at him with surprise. She had gotten so used to the professional, stoic side of law people, she almost forgot they had personal lives. Ones with skeletons in the closet like many others. But she wasn't there to judge.

"Passion can be the root of great and lasting happiness."

"And other things... like murder," Buck said.

Sheriff Cotton leaned forward. "Ben Franklin once said, 'If passion drives you, let reason hold the reins.'"

Diane tilted her head toward him. "You think passion is what took Irene Albertine's life?"

"Could be," the sheriff replied. "But I really think she pissed someone off so badly, they snapped. Let her have it."

Buck seemed to agree.

Meanwhile, the dart game heated up. A one-thousand-dollar prize was at stake. Hoots and hollers from onlookers almost drowned out the band. Diane craned her neck so she could see better. Small world. One of the players, Peter Osborne, from Cedric Hardwick's lab class, was taking his turn.

Laid back and enjoying himself, Peter was winning. He took aim at the board and fired off a dart that landed in the very center bullseye. Cheers, applause, and boos erupted, and he was brought up onto the stage to receive his prize.

Heading back down into the crowd, he passed Diane's table. Face aglow and spotting her, he slowed to a halt. "Hello, ma'am. Glad you came."

"Congratulations on your win," she said, echoing Sheriff Cotton and Buck.

"Thanks. It's a good night," he said and lifted his hands. In one was a check for one thousand dollars. The other was wrapped around a dart with the point down.

"Happy for you," Diane added cheerily. It felt good to see someone happy.

"You like darts?"

"Fun," Diane said.

"Sure," Sheriff Cotton said. "Used to play."

Smiling triumphantly, Peter winked at Diane. "Here's a souvenir." Peter raised his hand and brought the dart directly down, stabbing the wood table in front of her. She jumped and tipped the popcorn basket, spewing it everywhere. Peter, the champ, issued a curt salute, turned around, and wandered off into the crowd.

"He's drunk," Buck said, brushing popcorn off his lap.

Diane winced at the upright dart embedded in the wood. "Not if he made the bull's eye."

Sheriff Cotton rolled his eyes and pried the dart loose. "Jackass."

~ * ~

Being a Saturday, tracking down Dr. Andrew Granbury took a while. She found a note taped to his office door. "Back in office Monday morning, 10:00 a.m."

Diane retreated from Professor Row and stopped in the main lobby of staff housing at the center. A man was on duty at the small counter, apparently where shipments were received and residents called for guests. "Are you familiar with Dr. Granbury?" It was a strike in the dark as the visiting instructor could very well have a rental house off-property. Luckily, that wasn't the case.

"Certainly, ma'am.," the counter clerk said. "I'd ring Dr. Granbury for you, but he's out at the Hadley Ranch for the Pumpkin Festival. If guests are here in October, we suggest they go. We offer a shuttle to and from. You just missed one."

Diane got directions to drive herself. A back country road took her to a sprawling, white-fenced ranch in open ground. She turned off and drove under the gateposts with a wrought iron Hadley Ranch sign above. Luckily, she'd looked up Dr. Granbury's picture on the Institute's website and could find him more easily.

She found Dr. Granbury sitting at the end of a picnic table. His long brown hair almost touched his shoulders. He wore round-rimmed glasses and an outdoor vest over a denim, long-sleeved shirt. He was chatting with another man as she approached Granbury, introduced herself, and gave him a card. He grew solemn. "You're here about *her*?" His voice faltered.

"Irene, yes," she said.

He nodded briefly. "Later," he said and introduced her to the man with him. "This is Edward Miller. He's the archivist for the museum."

"Of course," she said and remembered him from when she'd visited the museum and watched the telling video of Set-Nohr arriving at Albertine's. Edward was middle-aged and wore a thick brown cardigan sweater over a grey crew-neck shirt. His black jeans had trouble holding in his waist. His broad face looked a bit harried to Diane, like the exacting nature of his work tested his patience. It was up to him to catalogue all the items in the Albertine Museum and maintain the database. But his tone and manner were friendly.

"Good to see you again," he said rising to his feet then reseating himself. Two box lunches with pumpkin stickers on the lids sat in front of them. "Join us?" he offered as Andrew got up and walked to a serving cart. He pulled a box off the top of the stack and brought it to her.

"Of course," Diane said and seated herself next to Edward.

"This is a benefit for the 4-H kids," Andrew said, and popped open the lid of the lunch box.

"We'll ride out to the pumpkin patch on a wagon and pick some to take back to the museum."

"Very reasonable donation," Edward said, zipping up his jacket.

"Margaret couldn't make it today, so we're here filling in," Andrew said.

Diane was glad she had grabbed her lined windbreaker before she left her suite. Autumn was definitely in the air. The sun shone warmly, but the breeze was cool. She had missed seeing leaves turning color. Moving to Florida had deprived her of rustling through them as she walked through the neighborhood park.

Looking around, Diane marveled at the property with its two-story wood frame ranch house with a cupola on top. Above it rested a weather vane. Old cottonwood trees, with their characteristic deep cut bark, stood on the north side. She could hear a creek babbling. Mountains stretched from north to south. About ten picnic tables dotted the manicured lawn. The gathering drew a nice crowd, all ages.

"Whose home is this?" she soon asked.

Edward filled her in. "Nathan Bridges, mine owner."

"Gold mine," Andrew threw in.

Edward added, "This area had several; most are mined out or closed. Makes for some interesting history, hikes, and stories."

Diane unwrapped a sandwich. "Mr. Bridges is generous to sponsor an event like this."

"Nate bought the ranch from the Hadleys years ago. This has become an annual event. He and his wife support the arts and the museum," Andrew clarified. "They're in the Osiris Society, and they were at the gala the night we lost Irene."

Diane locked eyes with him. Even now, he was forlorn. "You must miss her terribly."

Andrew drank cider from a Mason jar. "We were very close. We had plans."

"How did you meet?"

"At the center. I'd sat in on one of Cedric's classes, and Irene walked in. She sat next to me. We chatted during break. When she found out my line of work—paleontology—he showed me early ancient Egyptian images of birds and animals that were painted on walls in tombs. I took her to dinner not long after."

"Off to a good start."

His eyes flickered brightly, seemingly from fond memories. "We both were single and had interests in the ancient past. Hers were about Egyptian art, tombs, and mummies, and mine go back further to prehistoric North Africa."

"In the same zip code, sort of."

"But eons apart."

"Africa." Diane said thoughtfully.

"The continent is massive." Andrew raised a corner of his mouth and reached for a pumpkin muffin. "Months passed, and I wanted to propose to Irene."

"Was it mutual?" she asked.

"Completely." He removed the crinkle paper from a muffin and bit into it. "I'd heard later that Cedric had a serious thing for her."

"How much later?"

He looked at her soulfully. "Sarah told me about him after Irene passed."

"Irene hadn't mentioned it to you?"

"Never came up. But from what I can tell, Cedric moved on pretty quick."

Diane reflected on the sadness surrounding Cedric Hardwick's experiences with women. Loss of his wife, losing his dream girl Irene to another guy, and then how she lost her life. The double whammy must've drained him.

Edward lowered the lid on his lunchbox. "Listen, Cedric's doing okay. Student enrollment is up, and he's more focused on his work lately. The trouble he had with that suspended student has died down."

Andrew weighed in with, "That's good. Nobody wants to get tangled up in something like that."

A half hour passed, and Diane sat on one of the haybales loaded on the wagon. The horse-drawn wagon soon made its way out to the pumpkin patch. The dirt lane was rough, jostling her and the other riders.

"We can't pick pumpkins larger than we can carry," Edward advised Diane and Andrew as they arrived at a designated spot in the field. They dropped to their feet off the back of the wagon. Diane stood in a sea of pumpkins; mounds of orange dotted the ground off into the distance.

Somehow, her childhood had passed without picking pumpkins like this. But she'd carved a good amount of them. Her carved pumpkins usually had sported wide grins and with a candle inside. Suddenly, she wished Tom were here. He'd be carrying a large pumpkin back to the wagon with little effort. Keeping in shape went with his work.

Edward caught a call on his cell phone and walked away from Diane and Andrew. She kept her eye out for a small pumpkin to take back to the Nile Suite. Andrew wanted two, and they walked deeper into the field, away from kids, dogs, and grandmas.

"More about Irene," Andrew began.

"And your plans?" Diane asked.

"Precisely."

"Taking a trip?" she asked with an unsure tone, thinking it better not to reveal what Sarah had told her about their possible elopement.

"We were to go together. I'd heard about a new bone discovery from a colleague, Roger Graham. He found a Spinosaurus from six thousand years ago, and he wanted me to come. Around that time, Irene had mentioned something about a new excavation site she wanted to show me. Its location was fairly close to Roger's find, and taking a month away seemed feasible. She asked for us to keep it quiet for a while."

"How come?" Diane asked.

Andrew kicked aside a rock. "She never said, and I didn't need to know. But she'd been itching for a new resource to record the art for a new book she was planning. It looked to me like she'd found one."

"Whose tomb?"

Andrew half grinned. "Unknown, and that's always the question."

Pumpkin clutched in two hands, Diane was about ready to leave. "About Irene, had you noticed she was upset or disturbed about anything the day before she died? Bothered about something? Even on the day of?"

Andrew raised his chin. "Preoccupied. She was fresh back in town, and we had lunch that afternoon. She was preoccupied. But it was all about the gala. So much was involved. She wanted it to go perfectly."

For everyone's sake, Diane wished it had.

Thirteen

Threat Target

Driving back from the Hadley Ranch to the Oasis Inn, Diane stopped at the market for a frozen pizza she'd make for dinner. She wanted some time alone to work with her notes and crime board. She sharply sensed she was getting closer to unraveling some of the perplexing case she'd taken on. But no calls had come through from Sheriff Cotton today with any new tips, and Buck Dawson probably had gone fishing. Thus, she was still on her own.

She shopped and got back to the vehicle Max had arranged for her. The windshield wiper trapped a folded white paper against the glass on the driver's side. Hoping it wasn't a ticket, she plucked away the paper. She opened the door and sank into the driver's seat. She plopped her purse and the pizza box on the passenger's seat. Her hands free, she unfolded the note against the steering wheel with an oddly uneasy breath. Stark black words stared back at her.

Get out! Quickly, she looked up and saw no one, except for an elderly woman pushing an empty cart into the storage rack. Diane locked the car doors from inside and drove out of the parking lot. Her thoughts burst loose, and her pulse flew up as well as her speed on the road. She *was* being threatened. More boldly this time. She was somebody's target.

Reminding herself to put Pearl into her purse, she soon arrived back at the Oasis Inn. A quick call to Sheriff Cotton with the update triggered concern in his tone.

"You're catching heat."

"The good kind," she said, setting her hair free from her hairband. "The perp is more than nervous, he's afraid. It'll draw him out."

Sheriff Cotton harumphed on the other end. "With luck. Or he'll scram," he concluded.

Diane mused. "Maybe he can't scram."

"So, who can't? Rather, who is it?"

She repeated Andrew's question from earlier, "That's always the question."

A silent beat followed. "You free tomorrow?" Sheriff Cotton asked.

"So far," she said, thinking about tidying up the notes from those folks she'd already met.

"Buck Dawson found a guy who can tell us whether I'm sitting here with fake diamond evidence or not. You could come."

She warmed to the invitation immediately. "Time? Place?"

He supplied both and said, "Bring the note. I'll run it through ID for prints."

~ * ~

Later that evening Diane wrote the names on her whiteboard of all the people she'd interviewed to date. Each would have had the opportunity to snuff out the victim's life. Diane looked at each one as if they were a prime suspect and asked, "What would you gain from Irene's death?"

Max? Insurance money. Cedric? Possibly elevated status at Albertine's. Although he'd become a primary resource of Egyptology, he'd lost his love. Margaret? Freedom to love Max with no family disapproval. Sarah? Nothing; her tie to Albertine's was forever weakened. Caroline? Losing a friend for get togethers must be tough. Andrew? Sorrow and loneliness. Staffers like Katie and Mr. Roberts gained peace.

Diane still had to meet Louis in graphics, but Katie had pretty much filled her in about his difficulty with Irene over the gala invitations. They all had strained relationships with her. On the other hand, Edward had few complaints about her. Ben the room manager, and Randy the photographer had very little contact with her for issues to crop up. At least, to Diane's knowledge.

No one's frustrations with Irene struck Diane deeply enough for provoking murder. Still, there had to be some kind of unknown connection with Irene that had pushed someone over the line. Her dead body was proof.

She sat back on the couch and pondered the new errant question that flashed into her mind.

"Was Irene Albertine killed to hurt someone else?" slipped from her mouth. Ruining the Night of the Scarab Gala hinted at that. Max would've been the most vulnerable. So, who had it out for Max?

The possibility kept her awake late. It'd be another whole angle to explore. For now, though, she decided to keep on the direct motive path she was going down, day by day, person by person. Keep shaking bushes, readying for the culprit to fall out. Or, for someone to come forth with crucial, provable facts to turn this case around.

Fourteen

Time with Simon O'Leary

Taking a country drive south, Diane, Sheriff Cotton, and Buck found Simon O'Leary's modest home. A certified gemologist and a rockhound, he'd lined the gravel path up to his front porch with rocks. More unique ones sat on top of the rail. Buck rapped on the screen door and no answer came. Diane saw movement from the corner of her eye and walked to the end of the porch.

"Howdy," came from the side of the house. "Over here."

She leaned over the railing and caught first sight of Simon O'Leary. A tall, shaggy looking man, with hair combed by the wind and a beard almost down to his waist, gave her a wave. His craggy smile lit up his weathered face as Buck approached her side.

"Mr. O'Leary?" he called to the man.

"Most of the time, yes. But you can call me Rocky," he said. "Are y'all the law folks who can't tell a real diamond from a fake one?"

Sheriff Cotton showed his badge and replied, "Working on a case in Sandy River. I need your expert identification of a sparkly stone for a necklace we brought with us."

O'Leary dropped a rock on a pile. "Sounds serious."

"Homicide," Diane said.

O'Leary motioned to them. "Come on around to the back."

Diane followed the two men off the porch and along the side of the house to a back yard that sloped downhill to a creek. A small log cabin stood in front of them.

O'Leary led the way inside. Rustic and modern at the same time, the interior boasted long worktables and lab equipment, including microscopes, jeweler's loops, calipers, and stacks of round clear plastic containers. Various scales, tweezers, bottles of nitric acid, a testing stone, and cotton pads were neatly arranged near a high intensity lamp that shed light on the surface or through any rock, stone, or mineral that was presented for analysis. A Moh's Scale of Hardness chart hung on a wall and shelves held samples O'Leary had collected through the years. His college diploma and gemologist certification shared space on another wall.

O'Leary sat on a tall stool in front of a worktable and invited the small party to grab a stool for themselves to sit around him. He turned on the lamp and put on his wide-framed glasses.

"Let's see what you have," he said, ready for business.

Sheriff Cotton reached into his tan jacket pocket pulled out a plastic evidence tag with its number written in black felt marker. "There are two of these," he said. "Is this one real or fake?"

O'Leary's eyes widened at the sight of Irene's cartouche. "And where did this come from?" He pulled the bag from Sheriff Cotton's fingers.

"A market in Memphis, Egypt. Very old, and you'll find no karat mark on the gold. It's now part of the Albertine estate in Sandy River."

O'Leary nodded. "Of the Max Albertine Center? Saw on the news about their trouble."

Diane confirmed while O'Leary held the necklace up closer to his eyes. They warmed as if he were holding his first grandson for the first time. He pulled a digital scale toward him and gently laid the cartouche on top. "Four troy ounces." Next, he focused on the purity of the gold and worked with acid and a test stone to determine its karat content. When finished, he removed his gloves and whistled.

"My friends," he began. "You have an extraordinary and valuable specimen here. Solid gold, and..." He almost choked up. "I've never had the pleasure of seeing one of these." He tapped the brilliant red stone with tweezers and scrutinized the stone with a jeweler's loop. Moving the piece under the microscope next, he became motionless.

Diane and the two lawmen exchanged glances.

O'Leary suddenly looked up at them. "Bonafide red diamond," he declared. "One carat in weight, clarity—no occlusions, cut—perfect round, and color—blood red. Absolutely extraordinary," he crooned. "Twenty-two karat gold. D'you need a certificate of authenticity?"

Diane exhaled in relief. Max's gift to his daughter was safe and close at hand.

"Wouldn't hurt," Buck Dawson said.

O'Leary filled one out and handed it to the sheriff. "You said there are two of these?"

"A fake one was made for the owner to wear for every day. She used the real one for special occasions," Diane explained.

"The other one was stolen," Buck said.

O'Leary smirked. "The joke's on them, then... except for the gold. As usual, I'll send a description through the network."

"Network?" Diane asked.

"An unofficial stolen goods network. Guys like me help each other and the cops for finding stolen goods."

"Go for it," Buck said with Sheriff Cotton's approving nod.

O'Leary got up and crossed the room to a cabinet and opened it. He pulled out a purple velvet box and brought it back to the lab table. "Here. A piece like that deserves a better place to hang out in, not a baggie." He dropped the cartouche inside and handed it to Sheriff Cotton.

Cotton thanked him and said, "When I can release it, I'll see Mr. Albertine gets it."

Fifteen

Person of Interest

When Diane arrived back at Albertine's she ran into Sarah Fremont, Irene's personal assistant. "Do you have a few minutes?" Sarah asked. "Max has asked Margaret and me to go through Irene's things to begin clearing them away. I came across something you might find interesting."

Diane's curiosity kicked in. "Certainly. Give me fifteen minutes?"

"Let's meet at Irene's apartment."

She made it in twelve to Irene's apartment where she discovered the door ajar. Walking in, she closed it behind her and found Sarah amidst stacks of boxes and trash bags. She wore jeans and a sweatshirt and was holding an appointment book. "Margaret just left," she said. "She filled me in on some of this." She waved the book at Diane. "Let's go to the kitchen."

Diane followed and settled with Sarah at the small glass table centered in the room.

"So, what do you have?"

Sarah pushed the appointment book over to Diane. "I'm not sure. This was in the center drawer of Irene's desk. Irene and I used it to help keep her schedule. I'd opened it to browse through... sort of nostalgic, you know."

"Sure." Diane opened the book to a black ribbon marker. Appointments were neatly marked, mostly in blue ink.

Sarah pulled in closer to the table. "Have you heard about James Halifax?"

"Name doesn't ring a bell." She looked closer at the entries. "I see his name here. Who is he?"

"Hold on," Sarah raised a finger. "This goes back to just after I started working for Irene, two years ago," she began. "The Museum Gift Shop was needing a new manager because the first one was leaving. Max advertised for a replacement. Around then, Irene had gone to New Orleans for a scholarship benefit. On the plane she met James Halifax. A businessman, he was Irene's seatmate, and he was on his way home from an interview for a new position in Houston. She'd told him about Albertine's and the job opening. She was impressed with him because he'd managed a gift shop aboard a cruise ship, and later a curiosity shop in New Orleans. So, she felt he was qualified for running the Museum Gift Shop, and he applied for the position."

"A bit of luck," Diane said and smiled, but Sarah didn't.

"Meanwhile, Max had his eye on another applicant, Mr. Carl Roberts. College degree in business, and he'd been to Egypt. When Irene got back here, he told her he thought he'd found a strong candidate. Irene told him she'd found one, too. Max was delighted. She pushed hard for James to be hired. Margaret figured she had a thing for him, by the way. He was crazy about burial tombs. All of them. And their wares."

"So, two strong candidates vied for the same position," Diane said.

"Right. Max invited them here for interviews, and a third one, too. When James arrived here, Irene arranged to have lunch with him."

Diane looked closer at the entries. "Sure enough. Here's his name. They had lunch at Cactus Mountain."

"Very swank, down in the valley. And later, he came back just to visit Irene. See March twentieth."

Diane flipped to that page. "Lunch again... at Cactus Mountain."

"It's remote, and they offer prime rib. I made the reservations for them."

"Did you meet him?"

"Yes, and so did Margaret. He was good-looking, prematurely gray, and dressed well. He had a tat on the back of his hand."

"A tattoo."

"An asp, like in Egyptian art, and it curled around his wrist."

Diane winced. Not her idea of a tasteful fashion statement. Few inks were.

"Well, Max is no dummy. He'd interviewed James, and something about him sent up a red flag. He did some background checks. James had moved around a lot. His reason for leaving the cruise ship was that he got seasick too much. Margaret said Max laughed outright and thought that was rubbish. Then, Max picked our Mr. Roberts for the position."

"That has worked out, right?"

"Sure has. The Museum Gift Shop sales have doubled since he came on board. All was good, except Irene threw a fit over James not being hired. She even went to New Orleans to apologize to him."

Diane raised her eyebrows. "Maybe Irene did have a thing for him."

"I think James not getting hired nipped that in the bud." Sarah shifted in her chair. "Then, when she got back, she picked at Mr. Roberts a lot. But he didn't go to Max about her harassment. They'd yell at each other; but overall, he'd kept his cool."

Diane rested her chin on her hand. "Katie had mentioned there were difficulties with Irene. My hat's off to him for sticking."

"In time, Irene got better about it, but she never liked him."

Even so, Diane figured it was highly unlikely that Mr. Roberts went after Irene with chloroform. "Thanks for sharing."

She was about to stand up when Sarah said, "Wait. There's more."

Diane resettled as Sarah lifted the appointment book from the table and opened it to another page. "It's about this." She pointed to an entry further into the pages. "April tenth. Osiris Society Luncheon."

"Hmm. What happened there?"

"Nothing, but two days before, I was here with Irene. She needed help with her clothing." Sarah scratched her head. "She could put together deals for artifacts for the museum, but not coordinate her own outfits. So, she was trying on dresses and hats for the luncheon. Two men, wearing suits, came to the door and identified themselves. She let them in and asked me to stay. They were here about James Halifax."

Diane's curiosity soared. "What about James?"

Sarah's expression turned serious. "The gentlemen were agents from Immigration and Customs. They wanted to know if Albertine's had done any transactions with James. Irene told them they hadn't, and what was this about? The agents wouldn't say, but because they were from Customs it hit her. Irene yelled, 'James is a *smuggler*?' One dared a curt nod. She'd lost all decorum, and called him an S.O.B."

Transfixed, Diane could see why. "So, then what happened?"

"The agents asked if she knew where he hung out. Well, Irene could be a lot of not-so-fun things. But she was fierce about protecting cultural property and rightful ownership. She had no trouble telling those agents about her last time seeing James... in New Orleans. He'd taken her to his catamaran. 'You might find him on board the Cleopatra on Lake Pontchartrain.'"

That made Diane smile. "I wonder if they did."

Sarah resumed, "My guess is yes. Many months later, Max got it through the grapevine that James was awaiting trial. Then, just before Irene died, Max heard he'd gotten the bail money."

Diane shook her head. "I wonder who paid."

Sarah shrugged. "But here's the rest. Margaret swears she saw James here at Albertine's on the afternoon of the Night of the Scarab Gala."

Diane looked at her with disbelief.

Sarah raised her right hand. "I kid you not. He-must've registered, paid the three hundred dollars, but—" She waved her fingers in the air.

"But what?"

"He didn't come to the gala."

Diane asked, "Strange. He registered under his own name?"

"Nope. Margaret checked the lists. Invitations were first sent to members of the Osiris Society, and then the event was opened to the public for tickets. She thinks he might've registered as Dr. Harvey Bushell. That man never picked up his nametag."

"How interesting." Diane's mind went to work. Why had James come? Did he figure that Irene had helped the agents? Was revenge on his mind?

"Here's the best part: Margaret was sure the man was him because she saw his hand when he punched an elevator button. He'd dyed his hair and put on some weight. She notified DiNardo, but James was never found."

Diane squinted at the appointment book. "Does Sheriff Cotton know about this?"

"Max filled him in. Nothing has happened since." She stopped cold and tapped her bottom lip with her forefinger. Her nails were perfect. "He probably wouldn't like being locked up. You don't think he came here to do Irene harm, do you?"

Diane tried not to jump to conclusions. "I'll follow up with Sheriff Cotton."

That night Diane sat with her whiteboard filled with names of people in Irene's life. Many of them had reasons to dislike her; some had reasons to kill her. She added James Halifax to the list. She drew a blue circle around his name. A person of interest, but where was he?

Sixteen

Another Mystery Number

Fired up for more investigating, Diane visited Irene's office at Albertine's the next day. Correspondence, paid receipts, and bills of laden for countless artifacts for the museum laid on the floor. The phone blinked with unheard messages. A reply letter to Irene about the arrival date of Set-Nohr laid on top of a pile of *Egyptian Archaeology* magazines.

Overall, this office was more utilitarian than her personal office in her suite. She'd used a desk top computer versus a laptop. It, too, had been checked by the sheriff's office and returned. Still unplugged. Nothing seemed out of the ordinary to Diane, but she knew very little of acquiring ancient antiquities.

The wall calendar of the Great Pyramid caught her eye next. Irene had neatly noted times, places, and names in April's squares. Back then, her days were busy. However, she'd also made time to read. An Agatha Christie novel, *Death on the Nile*, sat on top of a Maya Angelou book of poems.

She lifted the mystery from the top, opened it and found a small bookmark tucked inside. She pulled it into her hand and gazed down at a fine drawing of a baboon. Turning it over, she found the back was blank--except for a handwritten series of numbers in blue ink.

24 48 44. Diane raised her eyes and blinked. The sequence was the same as the numbers hidden in the pen, which she'd snapped a picture of with her cell phone. Had she just found another safe combination?

She sighed. She'd yet to find the first safe. She opened her bag and pulled out her phone for another photo and took it. She scrolled back up to the first set of numbers she'd found days ago hidden in the blue pen. She tore the top sheet from the square notepad near the desk lamp, borrowed the gold pen from the desk drawer, and scribbled down the first set of numbers and the second set beneath.

Mystified, Diane stared at them.

"32 48 16 and 24 48 44," she read aloud. The safe combination idea wasn't completely taking root. "Whatever can they mean?"

The question plagued Diane into the evening. She called Tom and was lucky to catch him. She told him how unusual and beautiful the area was, and that she was gaining a sense of desert living.

"Send us a postcard for our office," he said. She'd started a travel board some years back.

"Good idea, and I'm still a coastal girl."

"Good choice. What else is happening? You sound tense."

She again admired his perception. "Today I found a second set of numbers. Twenty-four, forty-eight, and forty-four. But I've found no safes or combination locks for them."

"And the numbers were hidden like the first set?" Tom asked.

"They were written on a bookmark and left inside a book."

Tom said, hurriedly. "Puzzling. Give me a minute."

She did, and he came back quickly. "Those might be coordinates, dear. Hang on a sec."

Ten seconds ticked by. "If they are coordinates—north and east—they meet in the Mediterranean Sea, off the coast of Libya."

"The Mediterranean?" she asked in full wonder.

"Shhh,' Tom barked.

Diane next heard shouts from his end. "I got trouble here," he said and hung up.

More puzzled than ever, Diane shook her head. "So do I," she said to thin air. She'd just been handed another worry for her husband's safety and another piece of the Irene Albertine maddening unsolved case.

Determinedly, she went over to her laptop and googled the first set of numbers. Sure enough, the red flag icon popped up in the Mediterranean Sea.

"Just doesn't make sense," Diane muttered.

Irene was interested in land-based discoveries, not shipwrecks or drowned ports. Diane studied the numbers again and got some tea. Had she not punched the numbers in right? The first line she had given Tom and Googled was the first string she'd found. Another thought hit her: Maybe that first string I found was really the second string?

Coming back to the screen, she flipped the order and waited the few seconds for Google to work... and bingo! The red dot was clearly resting in Egypt, in a remote section of desert, west of the Nile, and about 12 miles from Edfu.

Diane's senses livened. Was this Irene's reason for spending more time in Egypt? Was this the location of the excavation in which she'd been interested? Did it fit in with all that had happened. If so, how?

For now, Diane sank into an abyss of questions. She yearned for answers from the people in Irene's world who had them. Surely, Andrew knew more than he was saying. Maybe even Max knew, and Cedric, too? Except, Irene had made the effort to hide the coordinates. Why? From whom? And how did she get them? Moreover, what did they promise?

There were major unsolved mysteries still alive today over the whereabouts of famous pharaohs' tombs. Even to Diane it made sense not to divulge findings until confirmations were determined about whose tomb archaeologists were uncovering. Had Irene been sitting on the whereabouts of the most elusive of burial tombs? Cleopatra? Nefertiti?

"Or am I thinking too big?" Diane lamented.

Seventeen

A Sketch of What?

Early in the afternoon, Diane arrived at the museum gift shop. Katie was on duty, and after finishing with a customer, she came over to Diane.

"Need a postcard?" Katie asked as Diane rotated the rack around and perused the different kinds. "These are by our photographer, Randy McPherson."

Diane found them impressive indeed. "I'll take three, and I need some cactus candy."

Katie led her to the specialty food section. "I'm glad you came in today. Something's come up about Ms. Albertine."

Diane leaned closer to Katie. "How so?"

"We received a crate from her. It came from Cairo. She sent clothing items, jewelry, and replicas of Egyptian statuary. It took more than months for the stuff to get here. She'd also included a separate package addressed to herself."

"Is that unusual?"

"Not really. When this happened before, she would come in to see how well things for the gift shop had arrived and to take her personal package with her. A manila envelope this time."

"Has the envelope been opened?"

"Mr. Roberts took care of it."

Diane glanced in his direction. "What did she send herself?"

"Mr. Roberts found a large sheet of folded paper with a drawing on it. Artful and practical. He said we'd have it framed to hang on the wall in our book section."

"A drawing of what?" Diane's curiosity soared. "Show me?"

Katie raised her forefinger. "I would, but it's out at the framer's studio. He's bringing it back today at three o'clock. Come back then?"

"I'll be here." Anticipation coursed through her.

"What kind of cactus candy would you like? We have plain prickly pear and prickly pear with jalapeno."

Diane chose one package of each for Tom. He liked it when she brought home treats for him. "Mr. Roberts needs to hold off hanging up the drawing until I see it. This case is still open, and what Irene had done is important."

Katie nodded. "I'll be sure to let him know."

~ * ~

Killing time until three o'clock, Diane drove to Sheriff Cotton's office. Buck Dawson's car was in the lot, and she found the sheriff's office door closed. She tapped lightly on the wood.

"Diane Phipps here," she said.

"C'mon in," Sheriff Cotton said.

Buck greeted her with a nod as she sat on the same chair she'd used before.

"Marshal Dawson here has some news," Sheriff Cotton told her.

"My fugitives turned up at Raphael's cousin's house while he was out." Buck stretched out a leg and crossed his chest with his arms. "They left a note. 'Sorry to miss you.' A neighbor saw them leaving in a white Ford 150 4X4."

"Plate number?" Diane asked.

"The neighbor got a partial from her kitchen window." Diane couldn't help but notice his frown. Buck had to be hoping for something more conclusive to help him bag the fugitives. She figured his search was just as intense as hers for Irene's killer.

"We ran it with what we had. Could be a stolen one from Walsenburg."

"So, what happens next?" Diane asked.

"We put an APB out, and they'll turn up," Sheriff Cotton replied.

Buck unfolded himself. "I'm sticking here. I want the pleasure of hauling them in."

"You deserve the honor," Diane said.

"Anything new from you?" Sheriff Cotton asked.

"Possibly. The museum gift shop received a crate from Irene."

Both men swung their heads toward her.

"She'd sent it from Cairo months ago. I'll be checking out exactly what she'd put in the envelope she'd addressed to herself and added to the crate. Some kind of drawing. Could count for something."

"Confiscate it," Sheriff Cotton directed.

"Yes sir. In progress."

Eighteen

Postcards, Peter, and Chester the Camel

Diane finished with Sheriff Cotton and showed up at the museum gift shop about ten minutes before three. Katie was busy with Peter from Cedric's lab. He was buying a pen.

"I need blue ink," he told Katie.

She checked the display. "These are black, so let me check in the back for blue." She left for the storage area, and Diane said hello to him.

"Hey," he said, recognizing her. "You still around?"

"Hmm hmm."

"Me, too. But I'm on Albertine probation. Limited classes for another three weeks."

Diane said, "Things change."

"You got that right. The bottom fell out of everything when The Stahlboard Foundation dropped me to the alternate list for an assignment. Delayed my life, my future, that's for damn sure. But I really like exploring ancient places, finding remnants of how civilization used to be. So, I got reluctant permission from Mr. Albertine to continue here, and he's submitting progress reports to Stahlboard.

I'm required to send in my own." He shook the pen at her. "On paper, signed in blue ink. My credibility is shot."

Diane spotted a postcard rack about fifteen feet away, but stayed in place while Peter sighed heavily and went on.

"Wouldn't be going through this shit if someone hadn't made a point of how I forgot my gloves." He rapped the unwanted black pen sharply on the counter. "I was asked to leave the room."

"That had to be rough," Diane said. "Did you resist?"

"Nope. I didn't want to deal with DiNardo in security. Nobody does. He's more than cranky; he's nuts."

"Nuts," Diane repeated dully. Knocking another person who upheld law and order raised her hackles. She felt them quiver.

"DiNardo wanted to cite me for going into the Luxor Ballroom weeks later after my trouble in class and on the day of that big-assed gala Albertine was throwing for the new, very old mummy." His face looked pinched. "All I wanted to do was look at her before the crowd hit. You know?"

Diane asked, "Were there No Admittance signs posted?"

"Not a damned one. I'd slipped in the main door."

"Interesting," Diane said. All of a sudden, buying postcards came second. "Anyone else in there with you?"

"Someone was up on the stage, behind that garish red curtain. So I went up there, too."

"And what did you see?"

"A very dead bitch... er, mummy," he said and paused. "Set-Nohr, she was called."

Diane took a breath. "Who else was up there on the stage?"

"Don't know," Peter said. "Gone when I got up there. Probably the room manager."

"What'd you do then?"

"Nothing. Looked at the wizened-up mummy and left."

"Same way you came in?

"Sure, and I ran into DiNardo out in the hall. He was putting up those gold posts with the red velvet ropes for traffic control. Asked me if I had an invitation to the gala. Told him I didn't, and he said I had no business being in there. Even though I'd been put on temporary leave, I told him archaeology was my business."

"What happened then?"

"Told me he didn't like my attitude."

Diane nodded.

"Well, I sure as hell didn't like his! He said I was this far away from getting an in-house security ticket for trespassing. He held up his right hand and spread his thumb and forefinger apart less than inch. Peter demonstrated. "I don't like to be pushed, ma'am, especially for no cause."

Diane shifted her weight from one foot to the other. The postcards were calling, and Peter's manner, whether he'd been distressed, or not, prickled her sense of grace. Something about him seemed raw, or unfinished.

He went on. "Anyway, when I got up from my lab stool, which was shaky as shit, I bumped the jar I was dusting for the exam. It almost hit the floor." He clapped his hands together once loudly. "Hardwick named a room monitor as he had stepped out for a phone call. He had come back into the room just as the jar began to fall. Felt like my life ended right then and there."

Diane regarded him quietly for a moment. "I hope the Foundation comes through for you soon with a job."

Peter stuck his hands in his jeans' pockets. "Unlikely. The alternate candidate list is long, very long." Resentment flashed in his eyes. "But it doesn't matter now, and I'm sticking here."

Diane raised her eyebrows as Katie reappeared.

"Here you go, Peter. I found blue pens." She handed one to him, rang up the sale, and processed his credit card for payment.

Turning to Diane, he said, "Later. Need to run. There's another dart tourney this Friday. Show up and be part of my spirit team?"

"I'll think about it." Diane gave him a wave, and he left the gift shop just as the framer was coming in with his delivery.

"Hi, Sam," Katie called to him. Carrying Irene's framed drawing cloaked in brown paper, he turned toward Mr. Roberts who was approaching the counter. He received it and paid the bill from the register while Diane and Katie moved the art to the storage room to rip off the covering. With two pairs of hands, it went quickly, and Diane was able to see the item first-hand.

Two sketches took up space on the paper that filled the wide wooden frame. Diane looked closely at each and the signature at the bottom. The camel drawn beside the name reflected the artist's sense of humor. "Chester" was scrawled beneath the camel, as well.

Remembering what Caroline had shared with Diane, she surmised that Irene's personal guide had done the work and even added a sketch of her favorite camel. Centered at the top of the paper, the notation appeared in script.

No. WN 251. Egypt Exploration Society, Principal: Private, U.S.A.

Spellbound, Diane pulled her cell phone into action from her pocket. She snapped a photo and repocketed her phone. Katie was excited with the outcome of the framing. "We will get offers on this," she said. "But it won't be for sale."

Diane laid her finger on the carved wooden frame. A fine job, indeed. But she suspected this drawing was way more than an artful addition for the museum gift shop. There was a story attached to it, and she wanted to know what it was. So much so, she said, "You can't hang this up yet."

"Why not?" Katie asked plainly taken aback.

"Not without a release from Sheriff Cotton."

Mr. Roberts ambled into the room. "What's this about Sheriff Jerry?"

Diane explained, "This drawing could be tied to the death of Irene Albertine. Sheriff Cotton wants to keep it at the station."

Mr. Roberts' expression registered disbelief. "How soon may I have it back?"

"Depends on what is found out about it. In the end, Mr. Albertine could claim it as part of Irene's estate. Aside from that, do you know what the artist had sketched? An excavation of a sought-after temple? A burial chamber?"

Mr. Roberts gazed at the drawing and shrugged. "Looks like a strung-out pile of rocks to me."

Frankly, it also did to Diane. But what were the curved shapes? Were they natural formations or part of a man-made structure? Certainly, experienced key people at Albertine's would know.

Putting first things first, she delivered the artwork to Sheriff Cotton an hour later.

"What's this?" he asked, looking up from his mail.

"The confiscated drawing Irene had sent herself. I don't know what it is about. But I'm feeling it fits into this whole picture. I have a photo of it."

Sheriff Cotton laid the framed art carefully on his desk. Bending over, he scrutinized the smudged paper and sketch lines. "Except for the camel, it's beyond me." He straightened. "You do the rest? Ask around. Might be important and might not."

On her way back to the Oasis Guest Inn, Diane thought more about whom to ask. Irene clearly wanted the drawing. What did it mean to her? Furthermore, would she want it shared with anyone? If so, with whom? Would it make a difference? The questions gnawed at her. This was tied to a homicide case. She sensed she should exercise discretion. But finding facts ruled, and they drove her work.

Tess Bridges, the librarian at Albertine's, might be able to help. She handled many documents, maps, original notes, and photos that were collected and assigned to the library for safekeeping and research. If not her, then Edward. He was the museum archivist.

Diane couldn't help wondering if Irene had expected to unearth a major discovery. Had she devoted her more recent trips because of it? Was the drawing she'd sent to herself part of her doings, or some other site of interest? For sure, she'd followed protocol for getting a permit from the proper authorities to begin an excavation. But were they considered classified? Finally, what was No. WN251?

Nineteen

Flowers!

Diane found Tess the librarian at the front desk. She introduced herself, and Tess slid off the high stool and came around to the front.

"I've heard you've come to help Sheriff Jerry and Mr. Albertine find out who killed Irene."

"This is true. I'm here to ask you about a drawing Irene sent herself. It arrived this week. Need a little help figuring out what the subject of the drawing is, and maybe even where? Thought maybe you could take a look at it with me?"

"I'm available for the next half hour."

"Thanks. Irene sent it back here because it was important to her. Anything that was important to Irene is becoming important to me."

"Certainly. Where's the document?"

Diane pulled out her cell phone and picked the photo of Irene's drawing. She handed the phone over to Tess, who pulled her glasses from atop her head down to her nose. She gazed at the screen with Diane.

"It's not a map, per se. More like a quick sketch of a section of an archaeological site. Undated, we can only assume the drawing and the dig is current. The paper is smudged, but it looks like a rock line, partly covered."

"With sand?"

"Most likely, and one set beside two others. Short patches of it. More needs to be exposed."

"Looks like a crooked creek, or a wall," Diane guessed.

"And long; one built for protection. But we can't assume anything."

Diane thought for a moment. "I'm wondering if you could look up some coordinates for me?"

"If it's in Egypt—"

"It is."

She smiled. "Then, we'll see mostly sand. Maybe rocks, or oasis by a river."

"Nothing specific?"

Tess removed her glasses. "We have maps of the Valleys of the Kings, Valley of the Queens, and pyramids, various temples, and burial tombs that have already been put on record. Nothing in progress, though."

Diane showed Tess the numbers, and, in a few minutes, Diane was again looking at shades of tan; an open, desolate desert on the screen. Tess's search supplied the same results as her corrected set for where the coordinates dropped. Not a hint of green or life.

"Is the Valley of the Monkeys nearby?" Diane asked.

"Not really," Tess said. She moved the screen way to the left and stopped. "That's here."

Diane raised her eyebrows. Another sun-dried open area, but with an unusual name, which she remembered Cedric mentioning. His trip was three years ago, and apparently had been a challenge. "Lots can happen in the desert," he'd told her. The photo of him with the small group of people came to her mind. She wondered if Irene had remembered the field trip the same way. Getting lost in a sandstorm must've had an impact for all who lived through it like sailors surviving a hurricane at sea. Had she shared the story with Max? What memories did Cedric carry with him?

Tess scrolled the screen back to the red dot showing Diane's coordinates. Again, she viewed vast open sand. Much green to the west closer to the Nile, and further south lay Edfu.

"Edfu?" Diane asked.

"Home of the Temple of Horus, and further south are more pyramids."

"Fascinating." But her mind skipped back to the open sand and the sketch. Were they somehow linked? Was it just coincidence, or was this Irene's future excavation site? No way to know, and she asked, "Do a lot of Albertine's professionals take trips for exploration, or to work at excavations already in progress?"

Tess nodded. "Three, that I know of. Mr. Hardwick was planning the first one for next spring. He wouldn't say where or for what. With all the trouble over Irene, he abruptly cancelled. I expect it was going to be amazing. Mr. Hardwick likes to think big, so it was promising. Even if it were a thimble, it would've brought him and Albertine's some new notoriety. He had even reserved display space in the museum. Mr. Albertine wouldn't have approved that space for tourist trinkets."

Diane figured not, as well. "Then, it's a loss, I suppose."

"Oh, yes. Bringing in artifacts discovered by one of our own is exciting."

~ * ~

Diane returned to the Nile Suite. Loose ends of the case swirled in her head, and she strongly yearned to make the right connections. She let herself in and found a note under the door. *Please come to the lobby for a floral delivery.*

She took the elevator down and walked over to the registration desk. Within minutes, Diane was opening a small envelope with her name written on it that was pinned to the bright orange satin bow. Flowers from Tom sped through her mind. Totally unlikely, but the thought tickled her. "Just because" was printed across the top of the little card. No florist's name was on the envelope. But it was the handwritten note inside that stole her next breath.

Save yourself. Leave now.

Diane pinched the card between her fingers and stepped over to the desk clerk behind the registration desk. "Excuse me, but who delivered these flowers?"

The clerk said, "I'm not sure, ma'am. I just came on duty."

"There's no flower shop name on the envelope. What flower shops are here?"

"We have none in Sandy River. Most floral deliveries come from Pretty Petals in Alamosa. But they have a big rose on their envelopes and their name. These might've come from the grocery store. Is there something wrong?"

Diane pursed her lips. "Nothing I can't handle." She carried the vase over to the coffee table by the settee. She phoned Sheriff Cotton. "I've received flowers... and another love note."

"You're getting popular."

"I'm getting closer," she said. "Any prints from the first note?"

"Still out," he said. "But I'll push it through. Bring in your newest."

"We have a whole glass vase for this one."

"Should help," he said. "Meanwhile, any new info regarding the drawing?"

"Tess at the library thinks it's a sketch from a new dig in progress near Edfu, along the Nile. I found some numbers which seemed to be coordinates. So, I had her look them up with me, and that is where they intersect. The note on the sketch is WN251 and is puzzling. I'm thinking it's a site number."

"Could be," Sheriff Cotton agreed.

"Big question is what would that site have to do with Irene Albertine? A deep enough connection for her to send herself a hasty sketch, or is it just a site of general interest? There must be plenty of those. Might it be from the site she had a deep interest in? It would make sense."

Sheriff Cotton took a phone call. "Yes, she's here. Sure, I'll give her the message." He hung up. "That was Max Albertine. He's put up a ten-thousand-dollar reward for any information leading to the arrest of his daughter's murderer." He paused. "To tell you the truth, we've exhausted the angles on this case." More than disappointed, he looked defeated. It was hard for a lawman to accept losing a war against a felon.

"You hang in, Sheriff," Diane urged him. "None of this is over yet. I can feel it in here." She tapped her head and her heart.

"I'm not cashing in," he said, raising his chin. "We never can. Just thought we could've wrapped it up by now."

"Cases and cats have minds of their own," Diane told him, half serious and half not. "Perseverance gets us through."

He nodded in agreement. "That, and a paycheck."

Twenty

Two Birds and Whodunit?

Two days later, Diane met Maximilian at the Lotus Courtyard. They sat on one of the padded benches and glanced occasionally at the video of Set-Nohr's arrival. He was disgruntled. A gold mummy mask, meant for the museum, was lost at sea. But his eyes lit up upon seeing Set-Nohr and the views of Irene on the screen.

"She was special," he said, gazing at her with a champagne flute in her hand. "Not a pushover, which Cedric regrettably learned."

Diane folded her hands in her lap. "Wasn't meant to be, I guess. But he has his work to occupy his mind and time."

"But not his heart."

Diane watched the screen. "I'm sorry everything turned out this way for you, Irene, and Cedric. Whatever I do won't be fixing it, except for giving you closure. But you seem to be holding up okay... and Cedric, too."

"He'd been through a lot before he ever hit our door," Maximilian said quietly. "Some bloke stole his wife--for money."

Diane shook her head. "Unbelievable. Ransom?"

"He couldn't pay, and they found her in the Thames."

"Must be terrible to cope with. Then, Irene passes."

"Cedric's very protective of all his possessions."

"It's all about loss," Diane said thoughtfully. "Hoping time will make a difference for him."

"Probably not," Maximilian said. "The wife incident happened about fifteen years ago. Still won't loan anything out to anybody. Figures he won't get it back."

Diane cleared her throat. "There's something I've been meaning to chat with you about."

"Go ahead."

She settled her gaze on him. "Another angle about this case has occurred to me." He waited.

"The killer not only took Irene's life, your closest and beloved blood relative, he also ruined the gala. He could've murdered Irene at any other place or time. But he did it so a lot of people would witness his work."

"You mean intentionally?"

"Possibly. It wasn't only an attack on her... it was also one on you. Essentially, killing two birds with one stone. So, I'm wondering who would want to do that? Any clue?"

Maximilian raised his palms and looked her in the eye. "I have no enemies."

"Maybe no *known* enemies, but somebody could have had it out for you two."

Maximilian stared at her. "Has Sheriff Cotton thought about this?"

Diane gazed back at the video. "Not to my knowledge. Hasn't brought it up."

"Who'd want to ruin me?" he spat, his face showing shock.

"And why?" Diane prodded.

Maximilian got up from the bench and stepped over to the fountain. The gold snakes feeding streams into the water glistened in the sun from the skylight. Diane joined him at his side. "We aren't always liked by everybody, Max."

"This goes beyond disliking me. This is about hatred, vengeance." He dragged his hand over his forehead. "How could this be? My business dealings are, and have long been, smooth. I set this place up as a learning resource center, and it's growing. And I set this place up for preserving early cultural history and invaluable artifacts. The fame belongs to Egypt. People who come here get a true sense of what early Egyptians were like. Who has anything against that?"

Diane couldn't say. But the possibility of dual targets and their staging intrigued her. One using murder, the other bringing a major event to its knees to hurt the host. All in one swoop. If so, Diane's scope of investigation just doubled. Maximilian's social circle was wide. It was mind-boggling, and another trip to the dunes might help her keep things in perspective.

~ * ~

Looking over her notes, Diane sat crossed-legged in the sand. The wind had picked up and she pulled the souvenir sweatshirt hood over her head. From where she sat, she could see what was left of Medano Creek trickling south. She'd learned that in another month it would be dry.

A few visitors crossed it and set foot onto the dunes at slow pace. One man headed her direction. Coming closer, he waved. She didn't recognize him. Not waving back, she unfolded her legs and crossed them at her ankles. She was hoping for some alone time, but the man definitely had recognized her. She dropped her notebook into her daypack.

"Hello," the man called to her. "Ms. Phipps?"

She untangled herself, got to her feet, and brushed sand from her seat. "I am. And you're?"

"Louis Millard. I'm the graphic artist for Albertine's." He stuck out his hand for a shake, which she obliged. "I stopped by to see you at the Oasis, but the desk clerk told me you were out here. Loaned you some binoculars for birdwatching?"

She tapped the daypack. "One of the amenities that comes with the suite."

Louis nodded. "Anyway, I thought I'd try my luck to try to find you."

Diane tucked her hands into the pockets of her jeans. "What can I help you with?"

Wearing an Albertine's windbreaker, he stood with his feet apart and hands at his waist. "Actually, I'm here to help you."

Somewhat winded, he plopped down on the sand and peered up at her.

"How so?" she asked.

"I know who killed Irene Albertine."

Diane stilled and squinted at him. From all appearances, he was dead serious.

He patted the sand next to her. "Have a seat."

She dropped down and settled. Partly from surprise, and partly because this might take a while.

"Why do you think you know who killed Irene?" This wasn't the first time someone had come to her with a killer's name. To date, none were right. But it was still worth a listen. Who knew what kind of useful information he had tripped over?

"Because it all fits together." He picked up a stone and rolled it around with his fingers.

"Okay." She put on her sunglasses. The glare off the sand was nearly blinding. "What all fits together?"

He tossed aside the stone. "First, this goes back a ways."

"I'm all ears, Louis. How far back?"

He seemed to relax a little. "Last Christmas; and it all started when Irene was in the wrong place at the wrong time... for somebody."

Diane turned her head toward him. "Was she being blackmailed?"

"Pretty sure not."

"So, where was she in the wrong place?"

"At the High Pine Lodge, about five miles from here. The Osiris Society threw a holiday party for members; about a hundred people come every year. Most of Albertine's staff also go, and the owners of High Pine Lodge have guests come. Mostly higher echelon folks around here—movers and shakers, political candidates, golfers, and the like."

"Irene was there?"

"In all her self-important glory," he said shortly. "So was Brett Washburn."

"Who's he?"

"Local contractor; built the Lodge from ground up. Anyway, his wife Wanda wasn't with him, but the word got back to her about what was going on."

Diane pushed hair back under the edges of her hoodie. "Was Brett being a bad boy?"

"To the max with one of the daughters of the guy who owns the golf course. Shelly, I think her name is."

"Lovely."

"Irene walked into the billiards room and found Brett and Shelly going at it on the pool table. Irene tried to duck out unnoticed, but Brett spotted her."

Diane lowered her sunglasses. "How do you know? Were you a witness? Or is this hearsay?"

He raised his hand for her to wait. "Hold on, there's more. Irene was murdered with chloroform, right?"

"Yes." Normally folks wouldn't know the means used in a homicide, but it had hit the local news a couple of weeks ago, along with another appeal to the public for information pertaining to the crime.

Louis rose to his feet and paced in a small circle. "So, here's the rest. I'm the assistant to the membership director for the Osiris Society. My job is to make the membership cards for new members. The cards are personally designed by me. Except for the formatting and logo, each card is an original etched on gold-tone metal and burnished to a high sheen."

"Sounds original and beautiful."

"They're keepers, for sure. I put a different Egyptian image on each member's card. Like Phil Moore's card has a pyramid, Winnie Holt's card has a mummy. There's a pharaoh's scepter on Jerome Bigley's card." Louis' eyes lit up with enthusiasm over each one he described. "I sketch the symbols from what we have on the property, or from photos." He stopped, moving in front of Diane. "About a month before Irene died, I wanted to use a lotus flower for a new member's card. So, I went to the Lotus Courtyard to sketch them. Doesn't take me long."

"It's a wonderful place."

"Indeed. I ran into Brett. He was showing one of his potential customers around Albertine's. We all chatted, and Brett got a call from one of his building suppliers. Apparently, it was his chloroform supplier to confirm an order he'd placed for it. Nathan repeated the order to the caller, and that's how I heard him." Louis ran his fingers through his hair and tried to smooth it out on top, but the breeze wouldn't let him. "I didn't think anything of it at the time."

"Probably not," Diane put in. "What does he use chloroform for?"

"It's a solvent, used for dissolving tar, resin, and whatnot. Anyway, it wasn't until I heard on the news two weeks ago about how chloroform was used on Irene. Then, I started to put two and two together." Another frown creased his forehead.

Diane thought for a moment and said, "Good of you, thank you. Frankly, we're stalled on this case," she confided.

"I'd have talked with you sooner, but..." Louis struggled to finish.

"Is there something else?"

Louis solemnly looked at her. "Irene went to the Osiris Spring Tea Party in June during one of her trips home. All women, and I don't know how the conversations went really, but Irene ended up telling Wanda about Brett fooling around with Shelly."

Diane cringed inside. Classic betrayal clashed with Irene, the whistle-blower.

"What did Wanda do?"

He shrugged. "She sued Brett for all he was worth."

"Then what?"

"Brett killed Irene."

Diane stared at him. "How do you know all this?"

Louis walked about five feet away, kicked up some sand with his foot, and turned around to face Diane. "Brett... is my brother. Technically, my older half-brother. Different fathers and no adoption, so different last names. We grew up under the same roof."

Louis looked consumed with visible grief. She walked over to him and laid her hand on his sagging shoulder. "Thank you for coming to me with all this."

He rasped, "I tried the sheriff first, but he's out training a new deputy recruit."

"I'll call him," Diane said and gathered her things. Walking side-by-side, they headed back to the parking lot in silence. Reaching his SUV, Diane said quietly, "Louis...

you've done the right thing. Sheriff Cotton will want to hear this directly from you."

"Fine. I just want to get past this. And I don't want to lose my job because of it." He thought for a few seconds. "Why would Mr. Albertine tolerate having a close family member on his payroll who killed his daughter?" He opened the car door and sank into the driver's seat. Opening the window, he said up to her beseechingly, "I love my work."

Diane found no words to assure him. Max could easily kick him to the curb. Her cell phone rang, and she answered.

"Yes, Sheriff Cotton?"

"We have a partial print match on the flower note you received. The first note was clean."

"A partial?" she asked.

"About twelve percent. Not enough for a match."

She held back a groan. "Well, I've got something here. Need to see you asap."

"I'm out in the field. My office, or elsewhere?"

"Your office. I'm inviting Louis Millard to join us."

"How about around lunch. Who's Louis Millard?"

"He works at Albertine's. You're going to want to hear his story."

"I'll order sandwiches from Millie's."

"No mayo, please. This guy is on to something. If it all checks out, he really might know who killed Irene Albertine, and why."

Sheriff Cotton whistled on the other end. "He's a witness? A witness would nail this case shutter than a barn door."

"Family member."

Sheriff Cotton's tone dropped into dread. "Damn. That can get sticky. Is the suspect local?"

"Yes."

"Do I need to pick up this informant?"

"Your call, but he drove out and found me out on the Dunes." She paused, then, "Tough situation there. Let's keep it low-key?"

"Absolutely. Mind if Buck Dawson sits in? He got a tip on the stolen white Ford pick-up truck. He'll fill us in."

Diane replied, "Certainly."

Twenty-one

An Alibi and About Chloroform

Ham and cheese on a French roll from Millie's took care of Diane's hunger. Sheriff Cotton's interview with Louis took care of her wish for a strong lead in the Albertine case. Getting a tip on the whereabouts of the stolen Ford pickup truck took care of Marshal Dawson's reason for sticking around. So, all in all, it was a good meeting at the sheriff's office.

Louis shared his theory, and an hour later the sheriff put out a call for the pick-up of Brett Washburn for questioning. Diane waited for his arrival. Apparently, he was up on the roof of the county courthouse inspecting flashing around a chimney. He didn't come down willingly.

Two deputies brought him through the front doors of the sheriff's building. Sheriff Cotton informed him of the reason he was there, to which he yelled, "I'm no killer!" He bumped Deputy Beard with his shoulder, and the first round of Sheriff Cotton's questioning went down-hill from there. "I wasn't even here on the day of that damned gala."

"Where were you?" the sheriff probed.

"If you must know, I was with Shelly. We were up in Cripple Creek. We went to a casino, won some cash, and drank beer. The Two Mile High Club was rounding up the donkeys for the winter like they do. We clipped a gray one with my truck. Shelly had a fit, and I got a ticket."

Diane, the sheriff, and Buck exchanged glances. She, for one, didn't want to hear about an airtight alibi. Thanksgiving was coming up in a few weeks and it'd be nice to be home with Tom.

"Then what?" she asked.

"We drove up near Mount Pisgah, and I proposed to Shelly." He smacked the tabletop with his palm. "Ask her. Just go ahead and ask. She's wearing my ring."

"Where is she?" Buck asked.

"What time is it?" Brett shot back.

Diane replied, "Two o'clock, Mr. Washburn."

"Then, Shelly's where she always is at two o'clock on weekdays."

Sheriff Cotton wrung his hand over his face. "You want to go home, Washburn?"

Nathan sneered. "Well, I dunno. You invited me here with these nice folks for us to talk. Now, you want to release me... out onto the streets of Sandy River?"

"Where's Shelly?" the sheriff demanded.

"No need to get riled up, Sheriff," Brett said. "I'm the one who has a right to get riled up. I don't belong here. I didn't do anything. I have rights!"

"You're also in the unique position to cooperate with this investigation," Buck put in and glared at Brett. "Again, where's your girlfriend?"

Brett leaned forward in the chair and folded his hands together. "Fiancée. Be nice to her. She's over at the old folks home taking Frankie around to visit everyone. He's a golden retriever trained to meet the residents at the home. Frankie gives them peace."

Diane withheld her smile.

Sheriff Cotton said, "You can rest here in our comfy holding cell." He signaled a deputy to go collect the woman. "We'll be checking your statement."

"How long do I have to stay?"

"Overnight. You'll have dinner and be out of the rain." He nodded at the window. Raindrops pelted the panes.

"Can Shelly stay with me?" he whined.

Sheriff Cotton sighed. "Not here."

"The sooner, the better I'm out of here, Sheriff. This is Thursday. Shelly and me always lead bingo for the Lions of Worship at the Sandy River Service Club. She doesn't like going alone."

The deputy began to escort Brett to the cell. "Wait," he said. "Who the hell said I killed the Albertine woman? Was it my ex-wife?"

"That's classified," Sheriff Cotton replied and nodded at Marshal Dawson. He reported on the tip he'd gotten about the stolen truck. "The plate was removed, so no positive ID on it yet, but it was spotted on an old U. S. Forest Service Road at the Dunes."

"Who spotted it?" Diane asked.

"A cell phone tower maintenance guy. The area was checked, and no trace of the truck. But Raphael will surface again."

Placated, Sheriff Cotton's eyes glinted with satisfaction.

~ * ~

Diane later added Brett's name to her whiteboard. Sometimes, a break in a case came in surprising ways and with little effort. Out of the blue today, Louis Millard had brought the choice morsel to her. All the destructive reasons for homicide were on the money. So, why weren't the bells and whistles going off in her head? She found out the next day with Sheriff Cotton's phone call.

"Yes, Sheriff Cotton?" she asked over her morning coffee. "Washburn's alibi checks out?" Her gut fell, and her intuition rejoiced simultaneously.

"Two reasons Washburn isn't our guy. Teller County Sheriff's Office confirmed a traffic warning was issued to him on the same afternoon as Albertine's death. His alibi is solid."

She set down the coffee mug and mentally went back to the drawing board. She pursed her lips. "What's the other reason?"

"It's about the chloroform. I re-visited the medical examiner's report. Irene's death was caused by respiratory failure. The report noted that the chloroform used was contaminated. Phosgene was present. I called the ME to find out more."

"Contaminated with what?"

"Time and a stabilizer. The stabilizer had been added by the manufacturer to prevent creating phosgene. In Irene's case, the chloroform used had to be packed with phosgene like fizz in a Coke. Apparently, the stabilizer doesn't work forever. Took around three years for the phosgene to build up."

Diane followed along. "So, the killer got his hands on an old batch."

"Right. Stored somewhere and turned bad."

"Stored where? At Albertine's?"

"Unable to tell. Bottom line is that phosgene is deadly-- with instant effect."

"Perfect for a killer with no extra time to spare."

"The thing is that Louis Millard overheard Washburn's confirmation of his order of chloroform--"

"Washburn's batch was new and clean. Unless, he had some old on hand?"

"He claims not. We checked with the firm for his ordering history. Millard overheard Washburn repeating his first and only order. But it doesn't matter. His alibi checked out. He was chasing donkeys in Cripple Creek.

"And, as a side note," Sheriff Cotton added, "chloroform's not the big knock-out drug everyone thinks it is. It takes a little time--more minutes than Irene Albertine's killer wanted to hang around for--*and* multiple applications for it to work."

"D'you think the perp knew that?" Diane asked.

"Slim chance," Cotton said. "More like pure dumb luck on his part."

Diane shifted her gaze toward the holding cell area. "Washburn's been released?"

"This morning."

"Then we're still on the hunt."

"For now, keep the faith. Persist. It's what we do best."

Diane couldn't argue the point.

Twenty-two

Past Woe, Today's Problem

Another few days passed and Max Albertine wanted to meet Diane again. She took her notebook with her. She was hoping he might've given more thought to the possibility that someone wanted to hurt him as much as they did Irene. This time he invited her to his suite. The private elevator delivered her directly to his living room.

"Come, sit with me," Max said. His casual appearance surprised her. He pointed at a chair for her to sit and chose the winged chair next to it. A low table separated them. "Please give me an update."

Diane settled where he wished and lowered her carryall next to her foot. Another surprise awaited her. There were practically no Egyptian art or artifacts in the room. Soft, low rock music was piped in from somewhere. A large chess set, pieces made from white quartz and obsidian, took up space on a glass coffee table in front of a long zebra-striped couch. A palm plant grew in a large ceramic pot next to a long table against the far wall. On it rested an oil painting of Irene. A vigil candle burned in front of her.

"Much has happened, Max," she began and opened her notebook perched on her knees.

"I have plenty of time. Please go ahead, and give me your thoughts, too."

Diane first relayed how she learned about Peter Osborn's situation and that a crate had arrived from Irene at the museum gift shop. She shared that she'd received a second threatening note, and only a partial print could be lifted from the card. She told him about how Louis Millard approached her with his belief that Brett Washburn had murdered Irene and why. Then, how that lead dried up with Brett's alibi. She passed along that Marshal Buck Dawson was still there and that someone had spotted the stolen truck that was tied to the two jewel thieves, and it was believed that they were still in the area. She also told him of how the sheriff, she, and Buck had visited the gemologist with Irene's cartouche, and that the real one was still with Sheriff Cotton."

"First, I'm glad you're safe and still here," he said. "Where's the fake necklace?"

"Not sure."

He fell silent, then abruptly, "You had asked me about anyone who might have a grudge against me, and I couldn't think of a soul. Then, this hit me the other day. I had an altercation a few years ago. I was sure it had all blown over, but maybe not."

Curious, Diane tilted her head. "A serious altercation?"

"Enough so that I lost a friend, Byron Cameron, over it. It was about intellectual property. We'd co-written a paper on secret passages, and it was published in *Architecture Magazine*. He picked up the ball and took it further. He elaborated on it and found a publisher and the paper was included in the work, *Ancient Boundaries*." Max pointed over to a bookshelf and Diane leveled her gaze on it. "He'd called the book 'my baby.' My name does not appear in it at all."

"Rather rude, eh?"

"To say the least. The book caught on in architectural and archaeological circles and even with the general public. Thus, sales were good. It attracted a screen writer, and his screenplay was picked up by a major studio, but it never hit the screen."

"Sorry to hear," Diane said.

"About two years went by, and Byron was invited for an interview about the book on the telly, which I happened to catch on the air in Dublin. I was there for an architectural convention focused on old stone churches. Small ones built by monks. Well, Byron took one hundred percent of the credit for the original paper and the book. I'd let it go. I had plenty in my life. I had my work, my wife, my daughter, and a sizable inheritance. But it was the principle of the thing that prompted me to contact Byron about the matter. He refused to forward me any royalties. He also plagiarized chapters that I'd personally written. That really upset Irene, and we sued Byron. The publisher paid up and dropped the book and wouldn't accept anything else from him. Which he still claims ruined his career and reputation."

Diane listened intently. "So, he expected you to accept all that?"

Max nodded. "He turned up at my office in Denver. Not for an apology, but to say 'This isn't over yet.'"

"What happened then?"

"Nothing. He dropped off the face of the planet. But about a month before Irene passed, I got a postcard from him sent from Hawaii. He'd ended up growing pineapples. 'Remember me?' was printed on the back with his initials."

"He was embittered?"

"Beyond belief, I guess."

Diane finished writing notes. "Had he been seen here at Albertine's?"

"No, he sent a 'representative,' Phil Quinn, from his pineapple company to help me celebrate my birthday, which remember, was on the same day as the gala. Margaret made him a nametag and added his name to the guest list. But all hell broke loose, and I never met him."

"How'd Byron know about your event?"

"Good question, but my family and I get mentions in various media. The gala was well-publicized."

"Open door for murder," Diane thought out loud, and Max's face fell. "I'll let the sheriff know about this."

Max nodded his thanks. "Another thing, Tess Bridges, the librarian, came to see me about a sketch Irene had sent herself."

"Yes, I figured it was important to Irene, and I wondered what the artist had sketched exactly. Tess sees a lot of documents and maybe she would have an idea. Do you know what it could have been?" She pulled her cell phone from her pocket and showed Max the photo she'd taken. "Tess thinks it might be from an excavation. I think it looks like a creek. Or a curved wall in pieces."

Max peered at it closely. "Definitely from a dig. Need to see more to know for sure."

"Was Irene involved with a dig?"

Max hesitated. "She was. I helped fund it. We kept it quiet until what was found was identified."

Satisfied, Diane sat deeper into the chair. "What's happened to the project now, now that's she's gone?"

"The work continues, of course. As her major donor, I get reports directly."

"I see." Her curiosity fired. "So, whose tomb is it? Someone noteworthy?"

"First, a dig season doesn't last long. No reports have come through for several months." He handed the phone back to her. "This sketch was taken very early on. Visiting the site gave Irene a strong desire to essentially file a claim with the authorities, which went through. The red tape takes months, during which she found a crew to work it. Her most recent trips had been primarily to check on the progress and see things herself."

"Well, this sounds exciting."

"It was... and still is. Dig season is back on with it being autumn. My next report should tell me exactly what she'll get credit for uncovering. Whatever, I'll be completely thrilled for her. We'll celebrate it here at Albertine's."

His eyes flickered with excitement. Diane felt happy for him. Unwanted stress was such a major factor with survivors of homicide victims. Any form of relief was refreshing and deserved.

"Looking forward to hearing what it is, too."

Max gave her a smile. "You're very brave to take on this case. You have a natural curiosity that serves you well in your work. It doesn't bother you to enter unknown subjects and topography. This place is nothing like coastal Florida. You also delve deeper into human nature, and why people do what they do, how they lead their lives, and you don't point fingers at people until it's required. Good on you."

Diane's cheeks warmed. "I can get frustrated, but I don't give up. Threats coming at me mean I've touched the perp's buttons. He's got a lot to hide, and I need to keep digging. That means I'm winning."

Max rose from his chair and walked over to the portrait of Irene. "If one believes in these things, I feel she sent you to me."

She pushed herself up to her feet. "Well, I need to find out who murdered your Irene."

Max shuffled toward the elevator. "I'm going for lunch now with Margaret."

"Enjoy."

"I do. Oh, yes. You might be interested in this. Cedric is offering a guest lecture on mummification in his lab tomorrow. It's a rare treat here at Albertine's. Open to the public. You could attend, if you like."

Diane picked up her bag. "Love to."

Max provided directions to the lab. Meanwhile, Max's story about a past enemy intrigued her. No angle could be ignored. Sheriff Cotton would want to research Max's ex-friend and his pineapple company. Would it turn out to be another goose chase? She figured the name Phil had given Margaret wasn't really his. His picture had to be part of the videos the photographer had taken during the event. The crowd was well-covered.

Again, Diane hoped a solid reason would rise for the homicide. For now, she planned to learn more about mummification under Cedric's tutelage. Ever vigilant for clues and connections, she considered attending the workshop all in a day's work.

Twenty-three

Mummification 101

Cedric's lab was full of people enrolled in Albertine's program. Yet, others like Diane, came, too. She sat near the front and scanned the room where Cedric spent much time. A bald, stuffed white dummy lay on a long steel table in front of the stadium-seating. Cedric used the portable whiteboard behind him for writing notes. He nodded at Diane and glanced at her often.

He started sharing the steps taken by Egyptians priests to prepare a mummy for the Afterlife. Each step took the process further in readiness for the body to be wrapped with long linen strips, layer by layer--up to thirty-five layers.

"The skin was washed with water from the Nile River. The lungs, liver, stomach, and intestines were stored in guardian canopic jars. Sand or linen was stuffed into the body to recover its human shape. Hundreds of pounds of Natron, a strong salt, were used for drying the body for forty days.

A student raised his hand. "What happened to the heart?"

"Stayed with the body," Cedric said. "Seventy days passed and the body was wrapped. Hands and feet first, then arms and legs. A pharaoh's arms were crossed on his chest. Gemmed amulets and shabtis were woven in with the linen bandages on the chest."

Another question was asked. "What're shabtis?"

Cedric ambled over to that side of the room. "Small carved funerary statues, often likenesses of those who served the dead person. They could be servants, a pharaoh's pets, and were buried with the body to help their owner be comfortable in the Afterlife."

Diane couldn't help admiring Cedric's smooth handling of the class and his knowledge. She relaxed and found herself taking notes along with everyone else.

"The mummified body was then placed in a decorated wooden coffin. Local woods like sycamore, acacia, or fig were used. Then it all was stored in a stone coffin and an elaborate mask was affixed at the head. The body was the soul's home. The mask would later help the soul find its body."

Cedric took more questions from the group as he showed photos and handed a ball of linen strips to a student to have a go at wrapping. Some of the yardage appeared to be stained.

"I was able to get some very old linen," Cedric said pridefully.

"Was it removed from a mummy?" a woman asked.

"Not so, and the resin stain like this can be dissolved with..." Cedric glanced at Diane for a nanosecond and went on, "with a strong solution. Now, let's wrap a mummy!"

The wrap didn't take long, with the helping hands of volunteers. Diane laid an amulet on the pseudo-mummy's chest, and it soon disappeared under bandages. When all was done, attendees strolled around the room to look at the artifact display Cedric had set up. It included tools, linens, photos, and a copper hook used to extract the dead person's brain. Diane found samples of sycamore and fig wood, and the kind of paint used on the coffins. A brown glass bottle marked 'solution' on a faded label sat next to a stone cutter and chisels. The canopic jar chest had its own space. Each of the four jars inside had a different cap, representing the sons of Horus.

Diane lingered and snapped pics of all. The final one featured Cedric behind one of the tables. He was in his element there and answered more questions as people passed by. As she moved on and turned to go, Cedric called out to her. "Wait up," and followed her.

"Congratulations," she told him. "This is all marvelous."

Cedric thanked her and asked off-handedly, "How's the investigation going?"

Diane held her bag between them and gave a general answer. "So far, so good. Every day I learn more about Irene and her world. It's quite fascinating." She avoided relaying how Max had encountered trouble several years ago that might have had lasting vengeance toward him.

Cedric said, "She was a busy lady. It's too bad she didn't get to see the outcome of her excavation."

Surprised, Diane stilled. "You know of her dig?"

Cedric's face hardened. "D'you know of her dig?"

An awkward beat followed.

"Yes. It's unfortunate she'll miss the outcome."

Cedric raised his chin. "We don't always get to finish what we start. On another note, those who're finishing our program are going out to the dunes to celebrate the end of this fall session. We're going out for a star party tomorrow night. The Orion and Lepus Constellations represent Sah, the Egyptian father of the Gods."

"I'm flattered you've asked. I'll try to make it."

Twenty-four

Button, Button, Who Lost a Button?

Diane found Sheriff Cotton in his office. The evidence box laid open in front of him on his desk. He was methodically going through it, studying each bag as he went. She took the seat in front of him and together they reinspected the items found in and around the Set-Nohr set-up and Irene's dead body.

"No prints on any of this," Sheriff Cotton said. "Evidence is our ally, isn't it? But nothing's happening here. No indicators that I can see."

The bag she picked up held the button. She opened the top and tipped the bag, letting the button fall into her palm. She peered at it much more closely than before. "I beg to differ. This is one... a button."

The sheriff didn't look excited. "Could've been on that stage for months."

Diane held it up for better light. "Hmm. A unique button, at that. Looks to be made from ivory." She pulled it closer to her eyes. "Lighter color on the front and darker on the back." She inspected the edge. "It's layered, see? And there's some kind of scratching on the top."

Sheriff Cotton opened his center desk drawer and pulled out a magnifying glass. "Here, this might help."

Diane tilted her head to one side. "Wait. It's carved, not scratched."

"What's it say? Is it an initial?"

"Nope. It's a carving of a bird. Not very deep. An etching, actually."

Cotton clasped his hands together and let them drop to the wood with a thud.

"A bird," he repeated flatly.

Diane moved forward in her seat. "Definitely, a bird. Also, this button is worn on the edges a bit. Been around for a while, I'd say."

"Around where?" Sheriff Cotton asked outright. "On an old shirt?"

"A sweater, probably. It's thicker and heavy-duty, with larger holes for the thread holding it on. No thread fibers, or yarn present."

Sheriff Cotton nodded. "Finders keepers, losers weepers. Whose is it?" he pressed.

"Good question," Diane said. "May I take this with me?"

He initialed the evidence record card and had her do the same. "Don't lose it."

Diane resisted the urge to reply tartly. She dropped the bag into her purse and tapped it with her forefinger. "I'll not. I promise. Meanwhile, I'm going back to the Luxor Ballroom."

Sheriff Cotton raised his hands and mocked a bow to her. Despite the disappointing outcome so far for this case, his sense of humor was picking up.

~ * ~

Finding Ben Rainier, the room manager for Albertine's, in the Luxor Ballroom was convenient for Diane. She arrived mid-morning, and the lights were on full. The room was being cleaned and reset. Ben's team had pulled away all the tables and the carpet cleaner ran full blast. Ladders were parked here and there under chandeliers that were being dusted. The fronds of the pseudo palm trees were being wiped down. The sound system delivered "Play It Again" by Luke Bryan via 93.5, the local country station.

Carrying a clipboard, Ben based himself up on the stage. Diane climbed the steps to meet him.

"Hey, Ms. Phipps," he greeted. "What can I do for you?"

Diane walked over to him. "Just needed to check with you on something, but you look pretty busy." She glanced out over the ballroom. "What's happening here?"

Ben, clean-shaven and his hair cut short, set the clipboard down on a folding chair. His sweatshirt sported the Albertine's logo, and the shirt fell loosely over his jeans. He stood over her by about six inches. He quickly threw a hand signal to a worker in the sound booth to turn down the music.

"We're getting ready for a new exhibit. Last year Max found an Egyptian chariot belonging to Ramesses II. It arrives in ten days. Another event is planned for it." His blue eyes shone with enthusiasm.

"When will that be?" Diane asked, rather surprised.

"After Thanksgiving," he replied. "We're picking up where we left off after the Set-Nohr debacle. Max is ready for it. He says we need to stick to our mission here at the center."

Diane silently agreed. Some families who had lost relatives due to homicide never really pulled their lives back together. It always seemed a shame to her.

"A chariot?"

"Used in battle," Ben added. "Some of the reliefs on the walls in here will be changed. The Osiris Society is lining up artists to do it. You should come if you're still with us." He left the last part hanging, almost like a question.

"I might be," Diane said. "I've come to ask you about something."

Ben gave her his attention. "What's up?"

She waved out at the room with a broad sweep of her hand. "I'm seeing how much effort you're giving the preparation for a special event."

"Yes, ma'am. We essentially start over. Every surface is cleaned, reevaluated for serviceability, and effects."

"I'm wondering about the surface of the stage." She pointed to the floor.

"That usually comes last. We want it to look as fresh as possible. The floor is vacuumed and mopped and rewaxed. We'll even refinish the wood if needed. That was done for the Scarab Gala."

"So, you're saying the floor was spotless?"

He nodded deeply. "Not a spec of dust dared lay on it."

"Would you say you have an eye for detail?"

He laughed. "I better have one, for this job."

She smiled and pulled the evidence bag from her purse. "This was found on the floor by Set-Nohr's coffin." She showed him the button. "The deputies spotted it, collected, and documented it. It was slightly wedged between two floorboards."

Ben placed his hand on his chest. "Well, we didn't miss it in the clean-up, I can tell you that. There was no debris of any kind left on the stage. I personally checked the condition of everything around three in the afternoon of the gala."

Diane stepped over to where Irene was found in the coffin. "Thank you. Knowing this helps confirm the presence of the owner of this button at the scene of the crime."

"You mean the killer?" His face contorted into a frown.

"I do. Apparently, this button was dropped or pulled off during the murder. Left unnoticed."

"Good grief. Whose button?"

Diane couldn't wait to find out.

Twenty-five

Falcons and a Prime Suspect

Wishing to buy earrings, Diane strolled into the Museum Gift Shop. Katie helped her locate them at a rear counter. She picked gold hoops with lapis lazuli accents. While paying for them, she noticed a stack of notecards near the register. A set of ten per box, they featured Egyptian symbols on the front. The top one caught her eye. A bird's profile took up most of the space. In black, it appeared to be a block print on the sand-colored paper.

Diane opened the clear package and pulled out the bird card. It was quite striking. She turned it over in her hand and found a description printed on the back.

Lanner Falcon (Falco biarmicus) ~ Sacred species for early Egyptians.

Represented the gods Horus or Ra, part man and head of the falcon.

The bird seemed similar to the one on the button. She plucked it from her purse and did a side-by-side comparison. Not an exact match, but close.

Diane left the gift shop with a heavy mind. At any other location, this could have been a vague coincidence. But logic told her the button belonged to someone with a taste for ancient Egyptian heritage. She had a strong hunch, stronger than ever, that Irene's killer was very close at hand... It was Sheriff Cotton's text that confirmed her hunch. The stolen necklace had been found.

~ * ~

Diane's drive to the sheriff's office was fast. Upon arrival, she heard voices and followed them to a room at the end of the hall. The door was open and the lights were on. She slowed her quiet pace, reached the doorway, and halted. The sheriff threw her a nod and motioned for her to come into the windowless room. Painted gray, there was no coffeemaker, and only two chairs on either side of a gray metal table. Except for the men inside and their clothing, the only warmth in the room came from them. Sheriff Cotton, dressed in his tan uniform, two deputies, and the wrung-out looking man who sat half slumped in one of the chairs looked at her. His dark hair looked longer than usual, and stubble covered his lower face.

A sole bottle of water rested on the table in front of him. He raised his wobbly, handcuffed hands, wrapped his fingers around the plastic, and took a swig. "Cheers," he said to her.

"Peter Osborn, what is this about?" she asked plainly.

He grimaced. "I didn't kill Irene Albertine. These... officers... are saying I did. That's what this is about." He jerked his hands back and threw the water bottle against the far wall.

Sheriff Cotton pushed the chair back and stood. "You're not doing yourself any favors."

Peter looked soulfully at Diane. "What am I supposed to do? You've got the wrong guy."

Diane sat in the chair the sheriff had just vacated. "Peter, you're in trouble here," she said quietly. "You wouldn't be here otherwise. You need to fully explain yourself. And if you can't do it with the sheriff, then you can tell me." The softness in her voice visibly calmed Peter. "What happened? I want to know your side."

Peter unzipped his jacket and sat straighter. "I didn't kill that woman. I honestly didn't. But, at one point, I would like to have done just that."

Diane arched an eyebrow. "At what point?"

"When she reported my glove mistake to Mr. Hardwick."

"How did Irene know about that?"

"Because she was visiting the class when Mr. Hardwick got the phone call he left the room to take. He made her the room monitor to watch us during the exam." He took a breath. "He came back in just as I bumped the jar. But I did catch it! She said right in front of everybody 'It's your job to uphold the lab requirements, Cedric. This needs attention.' Then, I was asked to leave the room. Very humiliating. That's when I vowed to make trouble for her in any way I could. But the bitch is dead. Good riddance." He rezipped his jacket. "May I go now?"

"Not so fast," Sheriff Cotton interjected. "There's the matter of the necklace you stole."

Diane resettled her gaze on Peter. "Want to tell me more? There is more, isn't there?"

Peter lowered his head and snapped it back up quickly. "I went into the ballroom. All I wanted to do was see the mummy. Wanted a picture of her. I went up those side steps along the stage, and it was kind of darkish behind that big red curtain. I made it to the center of the stage... and... and..."

"You killed her?"

"No, ma'am. I didn't have to."

"What do you mean?"

"She was already dead. Lying on the floor."

Diane widened her eyes. "Did you see or hear anybody while you were there? On the stage, I mean."

"Nothing. Just me, that dried mummy, and a fresh dead body." Peter shivered. "Kind of freaky."

Diane exchanged wary glances with Sheriff Cotton. "Shall we go on?"

He tapped the brim of his hat. "Be my guest." Folding his arms, he leaned against the doorway.

Diane turned back to Peter, who was rocking back and forth in the chair.

"I need more water."

Diane motioned to a deputy to give him another bottle. Peter unscrewed the lid and guzzled half of it down. Wiping his mouth with the back of his hand, he asked, "Am I done?"

"Not quite," Diane said. "Why didn't you call for help?"

"Because I didn't belong in there to begin with. I'd already had enough trouble at Albertine's."

Diane waited for more, then asked, "Why else, Peter?"

He hesitated and tapped his lower lip with his forefinger. "The necklace. I liked it. A lot. The bitch didn't need it anymore. It was on the floor, and I took it with me when I left."

Diane leaned back in the chair. So, there it was. What made perfect sense to Peter Osborn crossed the line of the law. He'd lost his moral compass.

"Where did you go afterwards?"

"To play darts at Millie's. I ordered the hamburger special. Came with pizza on the side. I felt rich with that gold and diamond. Didn't show it to anybody, you know. Just kept it right here. Wrapped up in a paper towel." He tapped his pants pocket. "It was a quiet chunk of change. Weeks went by, and my money was running out, and I needed to eat. I drove over to Rock Point and pawned it. The guy at the counter used a diamond tester and told me the stone was fake. That dumb bitch had given me grief again. But I got three hundred for the gold. I got by on it well enough until I got my next stipend check from Stahlboard. Even alternate listers get those."

Diane shook her head in amazement. "The cartouche is worth way more, Peter. Enough for Max Albertine to press charges against you for grand theft. Besides, you didn't try to render aid for an injured person."

Peter sat still. "I had no idea she was murdered," he said quietly. "She must've been evil to somebody else. And I'm still glad she's dead."

Diane whispered something to Sheriff Cotton. He raised a finger, turned around and pulled a file from a holder hanging on the wall. He rifled through it and handed Diane a photo. She flapped it down on the table in front of Peter. "You're saying you had no idea that someone had killed her?" The official crime scene document photo of the victim showed Irene's eyes were wide open and her mouth stuffed with a white napkin. "Why not?"

Peter pushed the photo away. "She didn't look like this when I saw her. She was lying on the floor, her eyes were closed and her mouth wasn't like that at all. There was no napkin, got it? She just looked dead, is all. Or maybe knocked out? No movement, no noise, no nothing."

Diane slid her glance over to Sheriff Cotton. "He's lying," he said.

Peter yelled, "No, I'm not." He banged his handcuffs on the table.

Diane decided to change tack. She pulled her purse up to the table and retrieved the plastic evidence bag and held it up in front of Peter. "Have you ever seen this?"

He shut one eye and studied it curiously with his other. "That's a button."

Diane took it out of the bag and held it in her palm. "Are you missing this?"

Peter reached over and touched it. "Nope."

As she pulled the button back toward herself, Peter snatched it from her hand and popped it into his mouth. Before his next breath, the two deputies wrangled him and one of them delivered a swift punch to the middle of Peter's back. His mouth flew open, and the button shot out, smacked the tabletop and bounced into Diane's lap.

Sheriff Cotton roared, "That's it. Peter Osborn, you're under arrest for the murder of Irene Grace Albertine." He signaled the deputies to whisk him away. "Book him. Without bond."

Finished there, Diane rose to her feet as Buck Dawson strode into the room. He took off his hat and exchanged greetings with Sheriff Cotton. "I've got another sighting report of Raphael and his girlfriend. Came in from a Dunes employee. Looked to him like they're squatting in a rough area. Do you have a deputy to do some drone work?"

A smile broke out across Sheriff Cotton's face. "Sure do. I'll put him right on it."

"What's been happening here?" Buck asked before he left.

Sheriff Cotton puffed his chest. "We've made an arrest. Got a call about the necklace turning up at a pawn shop, Rock Point, near Walsenburg. Picked up Peter Osborn for questioning. He's been booked."

Buck gave him a thumbs up. "Pretty soon we all can go home."

Sheriff Cotton turned to Diane. "Looks like you'll be back in Florida in time for Thanksgiving."

Diane closed her eyes briefly, hoping Tom would be, too. "You'll contact Max about the arrest?"

"My office is my next stop. Will call him pronto."

"He'll be happy. Good job, Sheriff," she said. His relief was apparent. "You should take a vacation. Come to Florida."

"Might go north, way north. Yellowstone."

Diane pressed her hand to his. "I'll email my reports to you before I leave."

"Keep up your good work, Ms. Phipps. Come back anytime."

Diane soon left the building with bittersweet feelings. Her time there was short. She'd done her job for her client, helped find the guy who committed another travesty on society, and got to see country she hadn't before. It was a good life. She would call Tom tonight.

For now, she'd go back to the Sphinx Café and have a little lunch. Then, she would change clothes into something warmer for nighttime star watching and head early to the dunes for a solo walk before checking in to the Albertine Star Party. Cedric would certainly make sure the ending of the fall session would be a major celebration. For sure, Max and Margaret would knock back some champagne.

Perhaps Diane would get a chance to relax and chat with Cedric, who had to be planning some kind of new adventure in the coming months. He probably had a bucket list a mile long. Most likely, he'd be returning to Egypt for another trip to the desert.

Maybe he would pick up his pending excavation plans? She never did learn why he had cancelled his last trip. Wishing good things for him, she got in her borrowed car and drove back to Albertine's.

She stopped in at the Nile Suite to freshen up. That done, she looked for her cell phone to check for messages before going to the Sphinx Café for lunch. She opened her bag. As usual, it was stuffed with various items. Her quick make-up bag, her small wallet with her ID, Kleenex, people's business cards, part of a Snickers bar, her notebook, Pearl, and other things a lady P.I. needed to get through her day.

All fine and good... until she spotted the small plastic evidence bag, which she'd forgotten to give to Sheriff Cotton. She laid it next to her on the couch and focused on the button. Her thoughts raced. Peter denied having seen the button. For a wild moment, she half believed him. She had watched him closely while he laid his eyes on it. When he first looked at it there was no flicker of recognition in his eyes. She sighed. Why he wanted to swallow the button puzzled her. Maybe to act out his anger for being hauled into the sheriff's office and held accountable for his theft? To generally foil an investigation? Or was he protecting someone?

That angle deserved more thought, and she stepped over to her whiteboard and wrote notes hurriedly. *Protecting someone? Peter found Irene unconscious or dead. Saw no white cloth stuffed in her mouth. Had Peter stumbled into a murder in progress?*

Finished writing, Diane sighed. She still had questions to sort out, including how Peter hadn't confessed to murdering Irene. Thus, things seemed unfinished to her.

Unless more facts rose to the surface on this case, the DA would have his work cut out for him to draw out more in order to convict Peter of murder. Without providing proof beyond a doubt, he might not even bring the case to court. Never before had she felt this unprepared to go home. But, again, the sheriff was satisfied. Still, she owed Max Albertine her best efforts; ones that would stand up in court so justice could be served. Max, then, would have complete closure. He deserved that much.

Twenty-six

Margaret's Dilemma

Diane was stirring sweetener into her iced tea when Margaret walked into the Sphinx Café and saw her sitting alone. "May I join you?" she asked and sat down opposite her without waiting for an answer.

Diane pulled her feet in closer under the table and smiled politely. Despite the pesky questions running around in her head, she tried to relax and enjoy some different company. If nothing else, she could admire Margaret's magnificent, thick cardigan sweater. The color was oatmeal and Egyptian Ibis were knitted into the front.

When Diane complimented her, she said, "We sold them in the Museum Gift Shop for a while. I couldn't resist."

"Good choice," Diane said. "So, with the program sessions coming to an end, how're you doing?"

Margaret let out a big sigh. "This has been the toughest year yet for me at Albertine's. If it weren't for Max, I'd probably pull up stakes and help coordinate events elsewhere."

Diane set down her tea glass as a server arrived to take Margaret's order. "Salad, my usual," she said.

"I couldn't imagine getting through what you all have had to deal with," Diane said. "Murder and theft and cancelled events."

Margaret admitted, "Worst ever time. But, in all honesty, I'm not missing Irene."

Interested, Diane asked, "You and she had differences?"

Margaret said woefully, "We didn't used to. But the closer Max and I got, the testier she became with me. I caught comments—everything from what I wore, my hair, and the room arrangements for events--the most important being the Night of the Scarab Gala. She told me I couldn't sit close to Max for any part of it. I protested and told her we certainly would be sharing the excitement through the evening. She threw a fit. She accused me of being a gold digger. Reminded me of our age difference. He's twelve years older than me. What could we have in common? she yelled one day. She was dead set against us being together. Irene wanted to control her father as much as she could, including his matters of the heart. I stayed mum for a long time, especially while I was at work."

"Sounds challenging," Diane said, thinking she could never handle spending day after day bowing to please such a person. "How long have you worked here?"

"I started not long after Max lost his wife. That was another rough time. He got depressed and threw himself into this center, which helped him level out again."

"How did you manage your dealings with Irene? To keep your professionalism?"

"I just laid as low as I could. Let her be queen, carried on without her acknowledging my efforts, and tried to stay out of her way. It worked... usually. At least, until she wrote me a note right after she'd returned from Egypt to be at Max's birthday celebration and the gala."

Diane adjusted her napkin on her lap. "A note?"

Margaret looked around for people sitting too close to hear their conversation. There were none, and she went on. "Very nasty note," she said, still lowering her voice to almost a whisper. "She said, 'Stop screwing my father and get a life somewhere else.' She even signed her name!"

Diane took out her notebook from her bag. "You don't mind, do you?"

"Not really. What's done is done. The best part is that I'll not ever have to hide from her or feel threatened by her again. She was a total terror."

"What did you do about the note?"

Margaret looked ruefully at Diane. "Well, I'd had enough of her tyranny. I saw her not long before the gala started."

"Where, how?"

"I looked her up to confront her."

"Looked her up?"

"I'd seen her go into the ballroom by herself. It was my chance to straighten things out with her. I couldn't wait any longer. I hadn't said anything to Max yet about what was happening. I was trying to keep him as my boyfriend. Even more... if he'd wanted that. Ratting on his daughter didn't seem like a good idea. It might've been enough for him to drop our relationship. Instead, I cornered her up on the stage behind that big red curtain. She needed to hear what I had to say... just her and me. Alone. The ballroom was empty, and that's all I needed to tell her to go fly a kite. Max and I were staying together no matter what she thought."

"Why didn't she want you to be together?"

"Because it wasn't her idea? I was good for him, and he was good for me, and that she had to deal with it. She had no right to do what she was doing, Ms. Phipps."

Personally, Diane agreed with her. "So, just to confirm, you were with Irene on the stage behind the big red curtain. And you heard or saw no one else up there."

"Right."

"Where was the mummy?"

"Where she belonged. Propped up between the top of her coffin and the bottom. She looked fabulous. I'd sat in on the meetings about the stage setting for the gala and still have the sketch plans. It was the biggest, most meaningful and prestigious event I'd ever helped set up."

Diane couldn't help admire Margaret's temerity. "I'm sure you'd never want to ruin that evening, for Max or the center."

"Of course not. It was his birthday, you know."

Diane and Margaret quieted while the server brought their food. When she stepped away, Diane probed further. "What happened up on the stage when you confronted Irene?"

Margaret let out a little whoop. "You should've been there," she said. "First, she was surprised to see me and immediately told me to leave. I waved her note at her and told her she had no right to interfere with her father's love life."

Mystified, Diane asked, "Then what?"

"She became furious. Her hair flew this way and that. She demanded I leave, or she was calling DiNardo." Margaret stopped for a fresh breath. "Just so you know, nobody in their right mind wants to deal with DiNardo. He's nuts."

Amazed none of this had been reported before, Diane stopped for some water.

Margaret continued. "Anyway, I stuck my ground and told her if she didn't change her tune, I'd be telling Max about her antics. That's when she shoved me. Hard. I grabbed the curtain to get my balance and almost pulled the thing down. I lunged forward and pushed her, and she fell backwards. Clunked her head on the corner of Set-Nohr's coffin. Her eyes rolled back in her head, like this," she said and demonstrated. "Then, Queen Irene dropped to the floor."

"What happened next?"

"I panicked. I couldn't wake her, and I'm pretty sure she wasn't dead. Just knocked silly and that she'd wake up again and leave on her own. I left the stage and used the side doorway out of the ballroom."

Diane finished the last note and looked up at Margaret with reproach. "How come none of this has come out before now?"

Margaret tilted her head sideways. "Max keeps his personal life private. His daughter was the reason I even went into the ballroom. To confront her. To me, all this was private." Margaret stopped and raised her chin. "Besides that, nobody asked me what I'd done the afternoon that Irene died. Except for this, I was seen about and taking care of the business at hand necessary for throwing a fabulous gala. A few hours later—when Irene fell forward out of that coffin—I lost it. All I could do was scream. Max, bless him, turned white."

Diane put down her salad fork. "This is another key part of the incident. I'll need to report this to Sheriff Cotton. He'll probably want to interview you."

Margaret straightened. "Am I a suspect? A homicide suspect?"

"Not so. But every little bit of information is important. Timing of things have become an issue. You've filled in some gaps for me. One last thing—when you left the ballroom did you see or hear anyone. Or did anyone see you leaving the ballroom?"

"Not that I'd noticed." She dropped her napkin by her plate. "Am I free to leave?"

Diane gave her a straightforward nod. "Of course. I wish you and Max the best of luck."

Margaret pushed herself out of her chair and ran into the server standing by their table. "Put our lunches on my account, please?" Turning on her heel, Margaret walked toward the entrance of the Sphinx Café, not turning back for a last look.

Diane sat in silence. Again, doubts crept into her mind that Peter Osborn's story was totally fabricated. First and foremost, Irene was still alive when he'd found her... and when he'd left her. He'd gotten what he'd wanted... a picture of a mummy and a fancy necklace he liked a lot. Not exactly a calculated, premeditated murder of the insufferable woman who had caused him major grief because of his lab mistake. But somebody else got exactly what they wanted: Irene Albertine dead.

Keeping her new thoughts private, Diane left the café and changed her clothes. She soon hit the road. Her spirits rose. How often had she had the chance to view the heavens amidst high sand dunes, much like those in ancient Egypt? Experts would be on hand to introduce her to the stars, the same stars that guided caravans and pharaohs to their destinies. According to Cedric, the great pyramids were aligned with three stars in Orion's belt. Orion, her favorite constellation, would never be the same to her after tonight.

Twenty-seven

Clever

By four o'clock, dusk was stealing light and throwing shadows over the rabbitbrush and sand. The dunes already seemed magical, Diane thought, as she pulled into the parking lot. Early as she hoped, she easily found a space and left the car locked. For extra protection against desert night temperature drops, she wore a jacket over her sphinx sweatshirt. She checked the star show flyer with its hand-drawn map to orient herself and began to walk.

Arriving at the trickling Medano Creek, she crossed the rivulets with ease and looked ahead. Off to the right stood cottonwood trees, and beyond that a thicket of brush that hugged a rock outcropping. She hiked that direction and spotted picnic tables loosely grouped and reserved for the star party. No one had arrived yet, and she grew restless.

She found a trail that would lead her uphill and past twisted juniper trees. Perhaps the extra elevation, away from light, would offer a new view. Half-way up she met Cedric. He, too, was layered for weather and wore a hat with a short brim. He deftly carried a telescope and tripod over his shoulder.

"You're early," he said, huffing from the incline. "Folks will start arriving in about ninety minutes. There's enough time to check out another place for viewing. Absolutely stellar." His eyes shone with anticipation.

Diane asked, "Is it far?"

He pointed ahead. "Just around those boulders and a quarter mile to the north. Most people don't know about it. Worth the extra distance."

Diane's legs were feeling the strain, but she said, "I'll give it a go. How do we get back down in the dark?"

Cedric tapped his day pack. "Headlamps. But there'll still be some light. Not to worry."

But Diane did worry. She was used to level beach walks at dusk with Tom. "Let's make this quick, then?"

"Planning to. I've been looking forward to making it back here. The evening star will be the first up. We'll be able to see it through the keyhole."

"What's the keyhole?" Diane asked, watching her step on the narrowing path.

"A round hole in the rock overhang near the old Horizon Gold Mine. The Horizon's been closed for about three years. The moon will shine through the keyhole by midnight this evening. About a hundred yards beyond that is Hidden Lake. Campers use it to get away from it all."

Determined to see more, Diane pushed forward. The view already stunned her. To her right, the dunes stretched out below her like a swirly blanket. The autumn sky would soon pale into silvery blue silhouetting the ridge lines from behind them.

She could understand how folks preferred this topography over ocean views. Making it around the curve, she slowed to a snail's pace. With his longer gait and speed, Cedric had gained about fifteen feet on her. The rocks shadowed them, and the world took on a different kind of natural beauty. Lichen-mottled rocks darkened, and the dirt under feet hid pebbles and divots.

Cedric halted. He set down the tripod, bent over a rock, and motioned for her to come see. "Here's a Western Fence lizard."

She arrived at his side and leaned down. "He's blue underneath."

"Indeed. We can pet their belly, and they fall asleep. But we'd have to catch him first."

"I'll pass," Diane said. Except for the anoles, or the pretty "greenies" that crawled on the side of her house, she wasn't a fan of lizards or snakes.

As she rose, Cedric opened his windbreaker to catch more air. She barely noticed, until his sweater caught her eye. Oatmeal-colored, beautifully woven and thick, its buttons snared her full attention. One of them was loose, hanging by a mere thread. She was about to call his attention to it, but stopped cold. The button featured a carved falcon on the surface. Another had fallen off, and its replacement had been sewn on with different colored thread than the others. She straightened and swallowed.

By now, Cedric was staring at her. "What's up?"

"Nothing. Just admiring your sweater. It's quite handsome."

She kept her tone admirably flat, despite how it was all she could do to refrain from pulling her daypack from where it hung behind her and drawing Pearl into full view. But she needed back-up, and she retreated into her thoughts.

All of a sudden, things made sense. Things she'd overlooked, like proxemics. Cedric had remained close enough to repay the heartache Irene had caused him. Oh, how easily he handled his disappointment over her refusal of his marriage proposal.

More answers stacked up, one by one. Why he'd stuck around and thrown himself into his 'work' at the center. Why he was so watchful of Diane while she sat in on his mummy presentation. How he avoided identifying chloroform in his talk, referring to it as a 'solution.'

So clever, this killer. Pulling wool over everyone's eyes. He'd even kept tabs on Max, feigning continued friendship. What better way to watch how the case was being handled, or how close the law was to figuring things out?

"I bought this sweater in the Museum Gift Shop," he offered. "It was the only one they had like this, with the falcon, I mean."

"Very unusual, I'm sure." Its buttons matched the one found at the crime scene. Without a doubt, Diane was keeping company with Irene Albertine's killer. Her breath caught. She had to think of something. She had to prevent him from becoming hostile. She'd even pet that lizard's belly to keep Cedric in place. Pearl was in her daypack.

Twenty-eight

TomTomTomTomTom

Diane's personal safety alarm went off in her head. Cedric stared at her; his eyes blazed with triumph for good reason. She deduced he had accomplished what he'd set out to do behind the red curtain the night of the gala. Moreover, he could leave Albertine's at the drop of a hat to hide in some part of the ancient world he'd studied so diligently. She had seen this display of innocence before; a classic cover-up for a criminal's deadly act. Like so many other killers she'd run into, he undoubtedly was so cock sure he'd gotten away with murder. Cedric Hardwick thought he had the perfect solution to ridding the planet of who'd hurt him most. If asked, he would say, "The world is a better place...and in some respects, is my oyster."

Diane's adrenaline soared, but she willed herself to appear as if nothing had changed. She'd learned how to put on a poker face from her Uncle Raymond on the Friday nights he'd visited her dad for a game or two. That skill had come in handy in her current line of work. Even Tom had told her she'd fooled him from time to time.

Cedric's stare hardened. He lunged at her and grabbed her neck with his rough hand.

"Cedric, what're you doing?" she asked, keeping up her ruse.

He wrenched her toward him. "You just *had* to ignore me!" he snarled. "I wrote you notes, but you're still here, you meddling twit. Poking into people's business, just like Irene." Malice glimmered in his eyes. For an average-sized man, he possessed gorilla strength.

Diane's thoughts scrambled. She gained some freedom of movement, lowered her head and bit his free hand. "You murderer!" she yelled.

Cedric hollered, "She deserved it!"

"You'll regret all this," Diane coughed out.

"Not any time soon," he said and tightened his grip. "She... and her father..." He choked over his words.

"What're you talking about?" she huffed as calmly as she could. She wanted to hear his words, his explanation. This was no time for wrong assumptions that could backfire on her or not hold up in court.

"That bitch STOLE MY LIFE. Those coordinates were given to me by Abdul during the sandstorm. They were entrusted to me, not to *HER*. Not to her father. Not for glory or profit. Exploring that location was meant for me. It was my destiny, and they robbed me of it."

Diane went still. "What temple do they point to?"

"No temple, you idiot," he spat. "The lost city of Amena-Ra!"

For a few nanoseconds, Diane felt a twitch of sympathy for Cedric. He'd been betrayed. His dream had been stolen by people he'd trusted.

"I get it," she said, "But killing Irene Albertine wasn't the answer. Redeem yourself. Serve your time and get back to work. Why not come with me?"

Cedric's face contorted into deep lines cemented with disgust. "Bollocks to that, madam."

Diane backed in closer and jammed her elbow into his solar plexus. He grunted, hunched over, and folded her in half from the waist down.

"You're dead!" he cried, stubble grazing her cheek.

His hand dripped blood onto the arm of her jacket. Her daypack separated their torsos. Unable to reach Pearl, she thrust her weight forward to pull him off balance.

Cedric countered with a fist slammed against her right temple. Twice. Dazed, Diane weakened. She blinked, trying to regain her vision. Tiny stars, of all colors, blazed behind her eyelids, but everything turned dark... and floated into cottony black.

~ * ~

Diane stirred, her awareness rising through layers of hazy awareness. Slowly, sensations returned, until she could call her senses her own again. She listened for sounds or voices and heard none. Her mouth had gone dry. She wiggled her left fingers and a foot with ease. Pain in her right arm stole her comfort as she lifted her eyelids. Diane gasped. She couldn't see a thing. Had she gone blind?

She was cold. Her head and her left arm hurt beyond belief. She slid her shaky right hand up to her temple to a solid lump. Disoriented, she pushed herself upright. Pebbles scattered and echoed as they hit the bottom of the pit. The air was still, lifeless.

"Where am I?" she murmured as her last memories filtered into focus. She winced. Cedric Hardwick had punched her. And then what?

She reached into her jacket pocket for her cell phone, but it was gone. Darkness surrounded her.

"Hello?" she called out weakly. "Is anyone there?"

No answer came, and fear flared. She looked around, hoping to find something familiar. Anything to let her know she'd regained consciousness, was still in this life, and in an Earthly place she could get out of. Alone and crawling, if need be. Her soft daypack had nearly slid off her shoulder, and still having it gave her instant hope. She fumbled with the flaps and found a water bottle and the tiny flashlight she'd usually carried for convenience.

Pulling out the penlight, she pressed the button. Its narrow beam of light captured craggy rock walls surrounding her. She followed them up, and up, and up. She pointed it downward to get her bearings. She'd landed on a collapsed timber beam tilted on a rock ledge. The edge fell away into a dark abyss.

"Oh, God. I'm in a pit." Her anger flashed. "That creep threw me in here to die. Help!" she cried out again. Nothing stirred. Not even a packrat, or a bat. But she stirred up a cloud of tiny gnats that swirled around her. She sagged frontwards onto the timber. Fear of falling, shock, fatigue, and the throbbing pain in her arm kept her in place. She suddenly wished for an Egyptian scarab beetle to keep her company. They were known for bringing good luck, hope, and protection, and she could use some.

She began to drift into sleep and thought this was the time for prayer. She'd been left to die while Cedric had carried through with his star party at the rendezvous point. For sure, he'd never come back to check on her. She coasted into a sort of brain fog and whispered, "*TomTomTomTomTom.*"

Time passed, but Diane was unsure how much. She was getting stiffer and stiffer as hours drifted by. She never expected to die this way, but it was beginning to look imminent. Hot tears from frustration welled up and were filled with resentment. She'd failed. She'd blown this case.

"Hello," she screamed with all her might. An echo made its way back to her. She pulled her jacket closer to her body for warmth. Water sips helped soothe her dry mouth. She turned the flashlight on and off many times and studied the rocks and timbers.

She couldn't see beyond the gap looming overhead. It had to be from where Cedric had dropped her. The edges of the gap were rough and more oval than round. Boulders assured her she couldn't move anything. The timbers were undoubtedly wobbly and as heavy, preventing them to be stacked for her to climb up and out. She eventually relented and relaxed as best she could. Waiting for help or death, whichever came first, seemed her only answer, and hunger was setting in.

She dozed again and stirred enough to reposition herself. Her imagination was kicking in because she smelled...coffee.

Twenty-nine

Help!

Diane swore the aroma was getting stronger. True or not, smelling coffee comforted her. For good measure, she aimed the flashlight beam straight up at the ceiling gap for the light to escape. A simple beam of hope.

Her arm ached mercilessly, swollen and useless. She cradled it with her other hand and drew it closer to her. Leaning her head back against the rock, she gazed up at the dark hole.

"Hello? Help me, please!" she called out one more time and closed her eyes.

Pebbles rained down on her. "Hello!" came back gruffly. "Who are you?" At least, it wasn't Cedric. "What're you doing down there?"

"I'm stuck," Diane cried. "Can you call Sheriff Cotton in Sandy River?"

"How'd you get down there? Are you hurt?"

"My arm, my head," she called back. Her vision had gone fuzzy, but she made out shadowed forms of two men through the gap. One of them held a big tin coffee mug.

The second male voice chimed in, "Just hold on."

Relief sprang through her. This voice she knew.

"Buck, is that you?" she yelled hoarsely. "What time is it?"

"Ms. Phipps? Holy hell, what happened?"

She sat up straighter. "Buck, go find Cedric Hardwick. He killed Irene Albertine. I was next." She paused, then said wryly, "I'll just wait here." Gosh, it felt good to laugh. A short, indiscernible discussion erupted above her head, followed by, "We're getting you out... now."

~ * ~

Two days later, Diane sat with Max, Sheriff Cotton, and Buck in the Nile Suite. While debriefing, they signed the cast she'd gotten at the hospital hours earlier.

"That was too close for comfort," Sheriff Cotton said, finishing up his signature.

Frowning, she nodded. "Tom agrees. He wants me to quit."

Buck signed next with a flourish. "All in a day's work." He gave her a thumbs-up for encouragement. He looked more relaxed than usual.

"How'd you find me?" she asked.

"A matter of luck. I was following up a lead from a Dunes worker. He'd been using his drone and spotted Raphael and his girlfriend up in the campground on the same trail as the one to the mine. Halfway up I met Nate Bridges, a gold mine owner. It was early, and he was sitting on a rock near the mine entrance having his morning coffee."

"Bless him," Diane said.

"He said even though the mine is closed, he still goes up. Takes pictures inside, goes down memory lane, and writes about it." Buck opened up a package of peanuts and tossed some in his mouth. "Anyway, I identified myself and asked if he'd seen any squatters lately." He told me it was hard to say, because the lake camp further up the trail drew people that stuck for a while. Then, he said, 'Hell, they might be holed up in my mine.' So, we went inside. About a hundred feet in we found a cell phone in the dirt.

"It's mine," Diane said.

"I have it," Sheriff Cotton said.

Buck went on, "There's a Y in there near the entrance. We took the right leg; the ceiling was higher than the other one. We went in a little further, and Nate told me the tunnel was hand dug and a lot of gold had been pulled out back in the day, and I'd heard water running and asked about it. 'An old waterfall; want to see' he said.

"I figured water would be important to Raphael and Zelda, so we veered off the main line and went there. All curves and slopes in there, and we came around a sharp turn, Nate said we were getting close to an adit. That's where the water was."

"An adit?" Diane asked.

"Yeah. It's a horizontal tunnel. He explained this one didn't have a vein, so they just stopped working it. We almost didn't go in, except he stopped and pointed ahead. 'What the hell's that?' he said. It looked to me like a light, coming straight up out of the ground and lighting the ceiling. That meant somebody was down deep in there hanging out."

"Thank God," Diane said. "I'd said my prayers."

Buck chucked another handful of peanuts into his mouth. "I was damn sure I'd found Raphael and Zelda, but instead we found you."

"Sorry to disappoint," Diane said, wrinkling her nose.

Buck winked. "When Nate and I left the mine, I asked him to call Sheriff Cotton to alert search and rescue to get you out of there." He paused. "How's your arm?"

Diane smiled faintly and held up her cast. "Better. This'll come off in six weeks. So, what about your fugitives?"

"We found them at Hidden Lake. Hair dyed and dressed like homeless folks. They even picked up a stray dog. They've all been transported to Denver."

Diane began to feel satisfied. First, she was safe. Secondly, Buck had found his fugitives, and Sheriff Cotton had released Peter and had the alleged murderer of Irene Albertine behind bars. No bond was posted.

"Any words from Cedric?" Diane asked.

"Enough for us. Says that when he'd applied for a permit to start an excavation, he found out that three months before an American woman was granted one for that exact location."

"She was Irene Albertine," Diane said, putting together the whole picture.

Sheriff Cotton provided, "Cedric wanted to kill her on the spot, but—"

"But she was in Egypt?" Buck asked.

"Right," Sheriff Cotton confirmed. "Then, when Hardwick further learned that Maximilian Albertine helped fund the project, it pushed him over the edge. He wanted to ruin Max for life. So, he waited for his chance to do it. Could have caused some real ruckus; he had access to almost everything at the center, including Irene's apartment."

Diane interjected, "But the gala gave Cedric the perfect opportunity to kill Irene and ruin Max's next big step to secure the future of the center."

"And ruin the guy's birthday," Sheriff Cotton finished. "Double payback. But he didn't expect Max to hire you."

Warmth rushed into Diane's cheeks.

"You made him nervous. Hence, the warning notes," Buck said. "Classic panic."

"And he locked me in the closet. A good thing, since I found the second necklace." A frown stole her smile. "But not a good thing that he dumped me down a mine shaft. I was never so glad to see men, a rescue basket, and a bunch of rope. It took them two hours to hoist me up out of there." She thought for a moment. "I missed seeing the stars with the others, but seeing the sun again matters more."

~ * ~

Diane spent the next couple of days packing and showing up for invitations to celebrate the arrest of Irene's murderer. The whole community could rest easier. While she was at Max's, the conversation turned to James Halifax. Diane was still curious why James had come to Albertine's on the day of the gala. Sheriff Cotton had some answers.

"First of all, the day after the gala, 'Jimmy the Runner' was involved in an accident on his way to Arizona and was apprehended. Also, in my further questioning of Cedric Hardwick about all that he did on the day of the murder, it came out that he'd met with James at Albertine's."

"About business?" Diane asked ruefully. "Under the table business?"

"Close, but not quite," Sheriff Cotton said. "Both collectors of antiquities, Cedric and James knew each other from long ago. They kept in loose touch, mostly in Egypt, over new discoveries and artifacts. Private collectors tempted James to bring some home under the radar screen, offered him good money to do it, and he went dirty. Eventually, his 'side business' caught up with him when a statue of Seti I turned up in Kansas City at a garage sale. Months later, the guy who bought it for ten bucks took it to the *Antiques Road Show*."

"Uh-oh," Diane said, feigning dismay.

"Took a while, but it was traced back to Halifax. A warrant went out."

"So, how'd James get out and about again?"

"Cedric paid his bail," Max provided.

Diane shook her head. "I thought Cedric engaged in reputable collecting."

"He does," Max said flatly. Diane could tell the mere mention of Cedric's name caused him grief. What a shock it must've been for him to discover Cedric had murdered Irene.

"But Cedric felt he owed James a favor," Sheriff Cotton said. "James got him out of a tight squeeze with a gang in London because Cedric was in the wrong place at the wrong time. James had saved his life. When Cedric heard that James was heading to jail, Cedric stepped up and paid his bail... on the condition that James would go clean from his first day out." He paused, then said, "Ironic, eh? Our murderer was promoting clean living."

Diane raised her eyebrows. "Most criminals also have a decent side. They're not bad all the time. But has James followed through?"

Sheriff Cotton stirred in the overstuffed chair. "Unknown."

"He called me and gave me his condolences about Irene," Max said. "He mentioned he was on his way to Athens. I wished him well and hung up." He waved. "And... bye-bye."

The next day, Diane said goodbye to Max and Margaret, and the Albertine Center for Egyptian Studies. Hours later, she arrived home ready for some rest and time with Tom.

Thirty

Case Closed

The day after Thanksgiving, Diane walked on Jax beach, heading toward the Pier. Tom stood near the end of it. She paid her dollar at the gate and bought a bag of popcorn. Wearing shorts and flip-flops, she adjusted her sun hat and passed assorted anglers. Seagulls strut along the tops of sun-bleached rails and eyed the popcorn. She tossed them some kernels. Further out, someone landed a flounder, and she slowed to look at its bulging eyes.

Tom was closer, arms rested on the railing. He was watching the waves rise and fall around the end of the Pier. A mesmerizing thing to do. The rhythm held him fast like it usually did her. He wore his khaki pants, deck shoes, cap, and sunglasses. It was good to see him relaxing, Diane thought. He'd arrived back home from his assignment four days before she did. Their neighbor, Kitty, and her husband Ed, had invited him over for dinner.

Kitty regarded Diane as a good friend, as Diane had found who had murdered Kitty's granddaughter, a professional mermaid. It was her first case in Florida, and being the first, Diane kept the file in the very front of her old Steelcase file cabinet.

Fresh home from the Sand Dunes, she reminisced about her sleuthing record as she walked. Going rogue had paid off; she took pride in her work. At first, when she lived in St. Louis, Tom hadn't wanted her to leave the burglary division to become a private investigator, or to operate on her own. Stalking cheating spouses wasn't her style. Diane was drawn to bigger issues, worse crimes, and saw the need for sticking with a case until it was solved. Bigger crimes meant deeper danger. She figured that's what had made Tom nervous. But after Diane solved the complex Thurman Cole case, Tom recognized she had a knack for finding whodunit. Afterwards, he supported her wholly. This was true, until three weeks ago when she had found herself trapped in a mine shaft.

He'd brought it up at breakfast this morning. "Are you sure about still doing all this?" he asked. "The turf is getting more treacherous, dear."

Diane saw the worry in his eyes, but bypassed it. Admittedly, she had to wonder if straddling a fallen timber on a ledge in a dark mine—being left for dead—was worth seeking justice for people she didn't even know. But then, Kitty Swan came to mind and how she'd found closure after Diane solved the mermaid case. To this day, Kitty watered the hibiscus when Tom and she were gone at the same time, often for weeks. Then, Diane's work became not just work— it became personal.

Yet, the answer about quitting evaded her. She sighed. Evasion never worked well with her.

It beckoned her to dig deeper.

Tom greeted her with a hug. The sea breeze ruffled his hair, and she could see her reflection in his sunglasses. She found signs of strain in her face. Lines were tighter, deeper, her cheeks less rosy. But her eyes still revealed determination.

"Let's head home for lunch?" Tom said.

"Leftover turkey?" she said.

"Works for me."

Arm in arm, Diane and Tom walked back out of the entrance gate of Jax Pier.

"I can hear you thinking," Tom said as they drove home.

She glanced down at her arm cast. He'd called it 'your badge of courage.' *But is Tom right? Should I quit?*

They soon arrived at their home in Atlantic Beach. As ever, the modest, one-story frame house looked good to her. Fronds from the palm tree brushed the edge of the roof, and her business sign requesting appointments almost needed repainting. "I'm just glad to be here," she said.

An hour later, Diane sat behind her desk, the Irene Albertine folder laying in front of her. She opened her desk drawer and pulled out the familiar rubber stamp and a red ink pad. She pressed the stamp against the red ink and swiftly stamped "CASE CLOSED" on the folder. Walking over to her trusty old file cabinet, she opened the top drawer and dropped the folder inside in alphabetical order.

In general, Diane liked order. Criminal cases represented disorder. Despite how things could never be the same, she did her best to restore order for survivors of those who caused chaos. The drawer was full, and it was a tight squeeze to put the Albertine folder to rest. She paused and gazed from the front of the drawer to the back. So many cases...

Yesterday, she had given thanks in prayer. And Tom did, too. Their respective careers sometimes sucked the life out of them, but they always bounced back. She sat back down and glanced at her yellow chintz chair, where potential clients sat and pleaded for help. Some from behind their tears, others angry over the injustice. Their lives had been shattered due to heinous acts, mostly murder of someone close to them.

Why people couldn't resolve their differences in a humane way was a mystery to them. Those who didn't or couldn't resolve their differences, created a trail of misdoings that deserved someone's proper attention to protecting society.

Diane gave it her all, quite happily. But had she done enough? Did the file drawer full of folders really make a difference? Had she helped curb the pestilence of destruction of peace and well-being? Had she deterred a future crime in some way? She certainly hoped so.

Soul-searching questions dove deeper in her quiet reflection. *What do I really want?* floated to the top of the pile. That answer came quickly to her.

"To be valued," she murmured to herself as Tom walked into her office.

"Mail's here," he said, dropping a small stack in front of her. His smile broke through her pensive mood. "Not to worry about quitting, dear. Things will work out."

"I'm glad you think so. We're in this crime-fighting world together. It'd be hard to stop."

A red padded envelope caught her eye, which she plucked from the pile. It held a note from Max Albertine, and also a small box with a gold scarab embossed on the lid. She opened his note with keen interest.

Dear Ms. Phipps,

It is with pleasure I write you to thank you for giving me peace of mind because of your role in finding who took Irene's life. I'm being assured the culprit will pay for his crime.

On another note, the sketch Irene had sent to herself at the museum gift shop proved to be fascinating. The curved lines are those of rock ridges that surrounded an ancient city, Amena-Ra, which was believed to be mythical. A mega tomb has been found!

I'm saddened that Irene will never explore its treasures. She had asked me to help fund this project, but kept the nature of it quiet... even from me. Indeed, I'm regretful over how she learned about the location and acted on it, which offended Mr. Hardwick. But I'll not apologize to him. My weakness, I suppose.

Finally, I've enclosed a fitting token of my appreciation of you and your devotion to my case. You deserve this gift. When the time comes for judgment of you, your dedication, and the risks you've taken for others, Maat, the goddess of truth and justice, will surely know that your heart is lighter than a feather. Enjoy the Afterlife!

Best,
Max Albertine

Diane opened the box slowly. Raising it up to her eyes, she tipped it toward her. Out fell a dainty, pure white feather. The plume fluttered down to rest on an empty case folder. She closed her eyes and opened them again. Tom was looking down at her. "You have tears in your eyes."

She handed him Max's note. As he read it, a knock landed on the front door. "I'll get it," he said and left the room. Minutes later, he escorted a middle-aged woman into Diane's office.

"This is Gracie Beckwith," Tom began. "She's visiting an old college friend here at the beach." She appeared distraught. Her oversized straw hat framed her fair face and complemented her cotton print dress. The large blue topaz ring on her finger sparkled as she clutched her woven purse to her waist.

"I don't have an appointment," she rushed to say. "But I need to see you. Something dreadful happened to my brother. He was found hanging in the boathouse. But Hank... our dear Henry wouldn't even kill time, let alone himself!"

Diane exchanged a long glance with her husband. Time stood still for a moment. Waving Max's note at her, Tom said, "I'll leave you two alone for now." He stuck his hand in his pocket and ambled to the door. "Go get 'em, tiger," he said and pulled the door shut behind him.

Diane glanced at the white feather and raised her chin.

"Nice to meet you, Ms. Beckwith," she said, opening her little notebook. "Please, come have a seat in my comfy chair, and tell me more."

Meet Karen Hudgins

Karen Hudgins loves good stories in all their forms. She began novel writing in the late 80s and is still going strong. She cut her teeth on writing seven single-title romance novels. In 2016 she began writing straight mystery novellas featuring determined Diane Phipps, P.I.

Karen lives in Colorado, is a grandma, and has a ginger cat. She engages in life-long learning and likes to cook for those who like to eat. Her hobbies include nature photography (botanical), growing flowers, playing pop/rock music on the car radio, reading, and hikes on mountain trails. She loves spending time with readers and her writing group(s). They all inspire her to use her imagination to write more stories. Karen is currently working on her seventh mystery novella.

Other Works from the Pen of Karen Hudgins

Murder at Marigold Mesa – Diane Phipps, P.I., devotes herself to finding out who poisoned the owner of a turquoise mine in New Mexico—yet, nobody appears to dislike him enough for murder.

The Kokopelli Caper – Diane Phipps, P.I., dusts off facts and digs for truth in Colorado and finds out who killed renowned archaeologist Dr. Ray McCormick.

Murder, Mayhem, and Monet – When a noted art restorer meets up with a Claude Monet masterpiece in Manitou Springs, her life ends abruptly—strangled. Diane Phipps, intrepid P.I. finds out who dreadfully whodunit!

Death of a Mermaid – Murder in Paradise? Diane Phipps, intrepid P.I., uncovers secrets, faces danger at Blue Wave Resort, and solves a perplexing case—the death of Mermaid Nerissa.

Blue Prince for Murder – Diane Phipps, P.I., solves her first case for an insurance company who seeks their missing wealthy policy holder and meeting their obligation to pay beneficiaries.

Secrets of the Heart – Molly, boutique owner, secretly believes she's fallen from grace and doesn't deserve goodness like compassionate Julian, master coffee roaster, who also has troublesome secrets–but brews up irresistible true love for her.

Dear reader,

I hope you've enjoyed reading this tale in another of
Diane Phipps' adventures.

Your opinion is valuable to other
readers like you,
who may be looking for books like mine.

Please consider taking a few minutes to post a review,
however brief,
on the site where you purchased this book
or on the Wings ePress web page.

You may also want to visit my author page
at the Wings' website, where you can find
all the other books in my series.

Thank you!

Karen Hudgins

Visit Our Website

For The Full Inventory
Of Quality Books:

Wings ePress, Inc

Quality trade paperbacks and downloads
in multiple formats,
in genres ranging from light romantic comedy to
general fiction and horror.
Wings has something for every reader's taste.
Visit the website, then bookmark it.
We add new titles each month!

Wings ePress, Inc.
3000 N. Rock Road
Newton, KS 67114

Made in the USA
Coppell, TX
30 March 2024

30733620R00115